Kilroy and the Gull

Other Books by Nathaniel Benchley

A Necessary End
A Novel of World War II

Beyond the Mists

Bright Candles
A Novel of the Danish Resistance

Only Earth and Sky Last Forever

Gone and Back

Feldman Fieldmouse
A Fable

Kilroy
and the Gull

by Nathaniel Benchley

Pictures by John Schoenherr

A HARPER TROPHY BOOK
Harper & Row, Publishers
New York, Hagerstown, San Francisco, London

Note:

It should hardly be necessary to point out that this is a work of fiction. The basic facts, however, have not been invented; virtually every item dealing with orca behavior has been taken from the published observations of a number of scientists, chief among them Dr. Paul Spong, whose chapter on orcas in Joan McIntyre's collection "Mind in the Waters" furnished the main body of the material. Those who might doubt the friendship between an orca and a seagull are referred to the International Oceanographic Foundation, which in the autumn of 1975 published a photograph of a gull playing tug-of-war with the tongue of a live orca, who seemed to be loving it. That picture, in fact, was the trampoline from which this book was launched.

—N.B.

I

On an evening in spring, when the ice was gone from the bay and the setting sun painted the smooth water a flaming red, the surface was broken by what looked like a cluster of sharp spikes, and a sound like escaping steam. Then the spikes were gone, leaving only ripples, and there was silence until they reappeared, again with an explosive puff. A pod of orcas, otherwise known as killer whales, was entering the bay, and from the shore they were watched by three men. Quietly, the men climbed into a moored launch, and waited.

"Don't start the engine yet," one of them said. "Wait till they get farther in."

The other two nodded, and began to arrange a large net in the stern of the launch.

The first man watched through binoculars as the orcas, surfacing every few minutes, moved up the bay, then he gave a signal, and one of the others started the engine and the launch moved slowly out from shore, its engine making a low, fluttering noise in the still air.

From far away the orcas heard the sound, and paused in their course as though waiting to see what would happen next. Then, as the launch moved toward them, they submerged, and came up several minutes later at a spot at right angles to their original track. The men in the launch gave up all attempts at surprise and headed full speed toward the pod, which vanished immediately, and, when next the fins appeared, there were only three, travelling in the original direction. The man at the wheel swung the launch around to follow them, but the first man stopped him.

"They're trying to draw us away," he said. "The rest should be coming back." While he was still talking, the third man shouted, "There's one! Two—three!" and pointed to the water off the bow, at the same time throwing the net over the side. The man at the wheel spun it around and the launch made a fast circle while the net snaked out astern, and when the circle was completed the net pulled taut and the water exploded into sheets of spray. "We got him!" shouted the third man. "He's a little one!" They had glimpses of a black body and white patches, and of thrashing black fins and snapping white teeth, and as they pulled the line tighter the young orca became more and more entangled in the webbing of the net, until finally he lay still, puffing clouds of vapor from his blowhole and emitting a series of clicks, trills, and squeaks.

"Let's get him to shore!" the first man shouted. "Here comes his mother!" He picked up a boathook and, holding it like a spear, waited for the large female that was circling the boat, whistling and clicking as she surveyed the situation. She made one run at them and the man stabbed her in the snout with his boathook, and after that she held off, trailing astern as her offspring was towed toward shore. Finally they reached

water that was too shallow for her, and she stopped, swam back and forth for a few moments, and then lay still in the water, making a low trilling noise.

A large truck with a derrick was backed to the water's edge; a sling was passed under the young orca, and when the enshrouding net had been cut away he was lifted into the truck, where two men covered him with wet blankets to keep his skin moist. The engine roared and the gears clanged, and the truck drove off into the gathering night, and slowly the fin of the mother orca moved out into the bay. From a tree nearby, an owl hooted with a note of maniacal laughter.

After an overnight flight in a cargo airplane, which was fitted with a sling and wet rubber mattresses, the young orca was driven to an aquarium, where he was lowered gently into a pool. He lay motionless, not caring what happened, and was only half aware of another occupant of the pool. Then a man jumped into the water beside him, stroked him and talked to him, and slowly walked him around the perimeter of the pool, to familiarize him with his surroundings. It was then he saw that his poolmate was a bottlenosed dolphin, which eyed him glumly and moved out of the way, but otherwise gave no sign of greeting. After two turns around the pool the man got out and returned with a whole salmon, which he held in front of the orca's nose. The orca wasn't interested.

"Come on, Kilroy," the man said, giving the salmon a little twitch. "Have a nice piece of fish." Still no response. "Kilroy the Killer Whale," the man went on. "You love salmon, and you know it. Here—let me

4

remind you." He jumped into the pool and, repeating the words "Kilroy the Killer Whale," rubbed the fish across the orca's lips. The smell was faintly familiar but the fish was dead, and unappetizing. "All right, Kilroy," the man said. "If you don't like it, I know someone who does." He looked around for the dolphin, flipped the fish in its general direction, and the dolphin rose in a glistening arc from the water and snatched the fish out of the air. Something in the sound of the snapping teeth awoke a response in Kilroy, and he felt a twinge of hunger. It was a long time since he'd last eaten, and a fish, even though dead, was better than nothing. He looked at the man with new interest, and the man smiled and got out of the pool. "I thought so," he said. "Wait a minute." He came back with another salmon. "Here," he said, holding it out. "Come and get it." Kilroy rose from the water, took the fish in one gulp, and sank back again.

"Lesson number one," the man said, turning away and wiping his hands.

Kilroy waited for the man to come back but there was no further sign of him, so after a few minutes he turned his attention to the dolphin, which was lurking at the opposite end of the pool. He swam across, and as he approached the dolphin backed away from him.

"Get out of here," the dolphin said.

"I wish I could," Kilroy replied. "How long have you been here?"

"Look," said the dolphin. "You stay at your end of the tank, and I'll stay at mine. Is that all right with you?"

"What's the matter with you?" Kilroy asked.

5

"I just don't like orcas, that's what's the matter."

"What have I ever done to you?"

"It's not you, it's the whole lot of you. You're a bunch of bloodthirsty bandits."

"Oh, come on," Kilroy said. "You're not making sense."

"You don't care whom you kill."

"We only kill to eat. And I haven't noticed that bottlenosed dolphins are exactly vegetarians. Are you trying to tell me you don't kill anything?"

"Only cold-blooded things, like fish and squid and all that. We don't eat warm-blooded animals."

"Like what?"

"Like my Uncle Ralph. He was eaten by a pack of orcas, and as far as I'm concerned the whole lot of you can go straight—"

"Wait a minute," Kilroy cut in. "Was he sick?"

"He was a little lame, but that's no reason to eat him."

"In other words, he couldn't keep up with the rest of you? He lagged behind?"

"Sometimes."

"Then whoever ate him was doing him a favor. He'd only have got worse, and been a drag on the whole group. Pretty soon you'd have had to feed him, and take care of him, and you'd all have been in trouble."

"Well, he didn't think it was a favor. He hated it."

"If you'll excuse my saying so, your Uncle Ralph was selfish. He got what was coming to him."

"You see?" the dolphin said, his voice rising to a shrill whistle. "You're all alike! You'll think up any excuse, just to be able to eat something! I'll bet you'd

6

eat your own grandmother, if you had the chance."

"I would not. Granny's the toughest one in the whole pod."

"That's beside the point. You'll eat your neighbors, you'll eat your cousins, you'll eat seals with the fur still on—you'll eat anything. I even saw an orca eat goat's fat."

"Why only the fat?" asked Kilroy. "Where was the rest of it?"

"Don't ask me. He was in the next tank over there, and I saw them feeding him this mess. I wouldn't have touched it with a ten-foot squid."

"Well, I've never tried it," said Kilroy. "But I see no reason why it shouldn't be good. All this talk about food has made me hungry."

"Well, you stay at your end and I'll stay at mine. I want nothing to do with you."

"All right," said Kilroy. "If that'll make you happy." And he turned and swam back to his end of the pool.

During the next few days, Kilroy suffered more from boredom than from anything else. He would swim around his part of the pool, inspecting the gutters and the drains and the inlet pipes and anything that happened to be lying on the bottom, and every now and then he had an urge to make a run at the dolphin just to frighten him, but he always resisted the urge and did his best to pretend the dolphin wasn't there. At feeding time the man would bring a big tub of fish and parcel it out between Kilroy and the dolphin, and any leftover scraps were immediately snatched up by a seagull, which seemed to know the exact time of the meal and would appear and wait by the side of the pool. Then, when everything had been eaten, the gull would fly away, and Kilroy would return to his end of the pool and try to think of something to do. He'd put his head out of water and look around, to see if there was anything he'd missed from beneath the surface, but it all looked pretty much the same: a series of tanks, and white buildings that shimmered in the sun, and trees in the distance. It was the dullest landscape he'd ever seen; the ocean was infinitely more interesting because, no matter how calm or empty the surface, there was always a great deal going on below.

At intervals the man would appear, bringing a collection of instruments, some of which he'd put in the water and some by the side of the pool. Sometimes one of the instruments would make a noise a little like an orca, but it was a poor imitation, and after inspecting it to try to find out how it worked, Kilroy lost interest. Sometimes the man played music through the machine, and this was a lot better, in spite of the fact that the music had a tinny quality that spoiled its tone. Kilroy was so bored he'd have listened to anything, and once or twice he even tried to make sounds like the music, but he knew it was no good and after a while he gave up. Once, as a joke, he went close to the machine and said, "The quick white squid swam over the surly plug-nosed dolphin," then swam away chortling to himself. The dolphin eyed him sourly from the other end of the pool, but said nothing.

While Kilroy was having his sessions with the instruments, another man was teaching the dolphin to do tricks. He'd hold a hoop out over the water, and if the dolphin jumped through the hoop he'd be rewarded

8

with a fish. Then he was taught to play with a ball, bouncing it in the air and knocking it through the hoop, and each time he did something he received a fish as a reward. Kilroy thought the whole routine was stupid, because he would have done any of those tricks for the simple fun of it, but to do that he'd have had to go to the other end of the pool, and he didn't want to make the dolphin any more unpleasant than he already was. So he stayed at his end, and watched the tricks with faint contempt, and every now and then muttered comments into the instrument that hung down in the water.

One day, at the end of the feeding period, the seagull stayed at the edge of the pool instead of flying away. With a long afternoon ahead of him and nothing to do, Kilroy decided to see what the gull had to offer. He swam across, and put his head out of the water.

"Anything I can do for you?" he asked.

The gull looked at Kilroy's mouth, and at his three-inch-long teeth. "In what way?" he asked, cautiously.

"Any way," Kilroy replied. "I thought you might be looking for something."

"I'm always looking for something," said the gull. "If it can be eaten, I'll take it."

"Well, I'm sorry, but we've finished off the fish," Kilroy said. "That was the last feeding today."

"You haven't quite finished it off," the gull told him. "From where I sit, I can see a lot."

"Where's that?" Kilroy glanced around, to see if he'd missed anything.

"Between your teeth," the gull replied. "They're a mess."

"Oh," said Kilroy, running his tongue over his teeth. "I know. It takes a while to clean out the scraps."

"Hold still, and I'll do it for you," the gull said. "That way, we'll both come out ahead." Kilroy held still, and the gull hopped down onto his lower lip and began to peck the pieces of fish from between his teeth. When he was through, he said, "Now put out your tongue." Kilroy did, and the gull explored the rest of his mouth. "I guess that does it," he said, at last. He hopped back onto the edge of the pool, then turned and took Kilroy's still outstretched tongue in his beak. "Honk, honk," he said, giving it two small tweaks. "I'll be back next feeding time."

"Thank you," Kilroy said, licking his lips. "That feels a lot better."

"Thank *you*," the gull replied. "See you later." He spread his wings, preparing to take off.

"What's your hurry?" Kilroy asked. "Stay around awhile."

"I can't. There's a farmer planting corn down the road a piece."

"What's corn? I never heard of it."

"You probably wouldn't. It grows out of the ground and makes food for people and cattle, but when it's planted it's just a small kernel, and birds can eat it. We line up and follow the farmer as he throws it in the ground, and pick up the kernels before he can cover them up." The gull gave a small creak of mirth. "First gull in line has his choice. After that, you have to scratch for it. It makes the farmer furious."

"Do you know much about people?" Kilroy asked.

"Enough," replied the gull. "Why?"

"I'd like to find out more. They interest me. Are they intelligent?"

"That depends on what you call intelligent. Look— if I don't go now, I'll find myself at the end of the line. We'll go into this another time. All right?" The gull spread his wings again.

"All right," said Kilroy. "By the way, before you go—what's your name?"

"You can call me Morris," the gull replied, and with that he ran a few steps along the pool edge, flapping his wings, and in a matter of seconds he was airborne. Kilroy watched him go and then sank back into the water, aware that for the first time since his capture he had something to look forward to.

II

When Morris came around next day, Kilroy was waiting for him. He'd saved a few scraps from the morning feeding and laid them in the gutter, and he'd had to keep other gulls away from them until Morris appeared. He concluded that gulls must have either a sixth sense about food or long-distance eyesight, because he had no sooner laid the bits of fish in the gutter than a gull appeared high overhead, wheeling and calling, then went into a vertical dive and arrived at the poolside with a wild flapping of wings. Kilroy snapped at the gull and it took off again, but this time landed a short distance away, and surveyed him in surly silence. It had been that way all morning, until Morris arrived. Then Kilroy let him have the food, while the other gulls jeered and complained.

"I have an idea," Kilroy said, when Morris had finished the last of the scraps.

"Just a minute," Morris replied, hopping onto Kilroy's head. "Open your mouth." Kilroy did, and Morris said, "I thought so," and began to pick bits of fish from between Kilroy's teeth. "If I weren't here to look after you, you'd have more fish than teeth in your

mouth. All right, now you can close." He hopped back onto the poolside. "What was your idea?"

"That farmer you go to for corn," Kilroy said. "Does he give you all you need to eat?"

"Are you crazy?" said Morris. "If I had to live on his corn, I'd starve to death in a week."

"Then who does feed you?"

"I feed myself. And if you think that's fun, just try it sometime."

"I've fed myself," Kilroy said, defensively. "Until about a week ago, I always got my own food." He thought back to his life in the pod, and it seemed like a hundred years ago.

"Yes, but you all hunt in packs," Morris said. "You zoom around and gobble up anything that gets in your way. There's no trick to that."

"It isn't all that easy." Kilroy was beginning to feel homesick. "We have to work for what we get."

"Try breaking open a clamshell, if you want work," said Morris. "You pick it out of the mud, fly over some hard surface like a road or a parking lot, then drop it and hope it breaks. Then like as not it's all dry and shrivelled, and tastes like an old sneaker."

"You've just lost my interest," said Kilroy. "I can't fly."

"Well, you know what I mean," Morris replied. "It's not easy."

"Then what *do* you eat?" asked Kilroy. "I mean, to keep alive."

"Anything and everything. Every day I have a regular beat. I start off looking for anything that may have washed up on the shore during the night, then check

14

the fishing boats to see if anyone's cleaning fish, then around midmorning go to the dump and see if any new garbage has arrived, then come here for the noon meal, then check the farmer to see what he's planting, then make a tour of the restaurants in town for any open garbage cans, then back to the incoming fishing boats, then another check of the shore, then back here for the last feeding, then a general tour of the vicinity, then off to the roosting area at sundown. It makes into a long day."

"I've been wondering about your eyesight," said Kilroy. "Can you see very far?"

"That depends on what you mean by far. I can spot a sardine from a rooftop, but for whitebait I'd have to be a little closer. But you don't always have to see it. Sometimes you just know it's there."

"How?"

Morris shrugged, and ruffled his feathers. "Search me. Smell, maybe; I don't know. Now, about this idea of yours," he said. "We seem to have got off the track."

"Well, I was thinking," Kilroy said, choosing his words with care, "or, rather, I was wondering, if I were to put some of my food aside for you each day, if that would be enough so you wouldn't have to go hunt for more."

"That depends on how much you put aside," Morris replied. "But why deprive yourself? What's in it for you?"

"I'm lonely, that's all," said Kilroy. "Lonely, and bored. I'd like someone to talk to, and—well, you know. Pass the time of day. Living with this dolphin is like living with a big snapping turtle."

"I heard that," said the dolphin, from the other end of the pool. "You leave me out of this."

"You see what I mean?" Kilroy went on. "Sometimes I'm tempted to go over and take a bite out of him, just to shut him up. The only trouble is, the people would probably object."

"You lay one tooth on me and I'll scream the place down," the dolphin said, in a shrill whistle. "I knew the minute I saw you you meant trouble, and you've done nothing to prove me wrong. All orcas should be drowned at birth."

"It's easy to see why your Uncle Ralph got eaten," Kilroy replied. "If he was anything like you, it's a wonder his own kind could stand him."

"You're just trying to start a fight," the dolphin said. "You're looking for an excuse to attack me."

"If I needed an excuse I'd have had one long ago," Kilroy told him. Then he turned back to Morris. "What about it?" he said. "Do you think you can live on what I leave out?"

"Frankly, no," Morris replied. "I could stuff myself to the point where I could barely fly, and an hour later I'd be hungry again. My system needs to keep the food coming."

There was a short silence. "Well, it was just an idea," Kilroy said, at last.

"I'll tell you what, though," Morris said, sensing Kilroy's disappointment. "I'll come by more often, and maybe bring some food with me, and that way we'll be able to have more time to talk."

"That'll be fine," Kilroy said, brightening. "Anything will be better than just floating here."

"Good. I'll see you in a little while." Morris spread his wings to take off, then saw something that gave him an idea. He went to the gravel walk that surrounded the pool, picked up a round, white pebble in his beak, and rose into the air. Then he circled over the pool and, when the dolphin came up for air, he let the pebble drop. "Bombs away!" he shrieked, as the pebble bounced off the dolphin's head and plopped into the water. "Scratch one bottlenose!" He flew away, braying with laughter, while the dolphin plunged about in angry, futile circles.

Later, while Kilroy was trying to think of something to do, a man came to the poolside and lowered an instrument into the water. Kilroy drifted over to inspect it, and was startled to hear his own voice saying, "The quick white squid swam over the surly plug-nosed dolphin." He looked carefully at the instrument, searching for an explanation of the voice which, while unmistakably his, was still not quite right. Then he heard, "I could do that one backward," followed by, "And for this he gets a fish?" and he realized he was listening to the comments he'd made while the dolphin was doing tricks. The whole thing was astonishing, and it could only mean that the man had some way of capturing his voice and then making it repeat itself. Kilroy backed away and put his head out of the water, in order to see more clearly. The man smiled at him, and said, "What did you think of that?" and after a moment Kilroy sank back beneath the surface. Here was something that needed a little closer investigation. He and the man had no language in common, but he sensed that something had passed between them that, with some care and effort, might result in a substitute for language. The idea was fascinating, and he swam quickly back and forth, clicking and whistling, while he tried to think of a way to approach the problem. The man reached into the water to retrieve the instrument, and Kilroy darted toward him, mouth open, to try to keep it from being taken away. The man snatched his hands back so fast he almost fell over backward, and Kilroy, who had grasped the instrument lightly in his teeth, was so surprised that he let it go, and the man grabbed it out of the water. It occurred to him that the man was afraid of him, and he found this odd because he'd meant no harm to anyone; he'd only wanted to keep the game going. The man gathered up his gear and scurried away, leaving Kilroy alone and perplexed.

Morris came by an hour or so later, bringing with him a fish head that had seen better days. He set it in the gutter, examined it, and began to pick at what little bits of flesh were left.

"What do you know about people?" Kilroy asked him.

"What do you want to know?" Morris replied, tugging at a shrivelled piece of gill.

"I want to know what they are—what they want—what makes them go. Just for instance, why are they afraid of me?"

"That's easy," said Morris. "Have you ever seen your teeth?"

"No, but I've seen other orcas'. There's no reason

18

to be afraid of me just because I have big teeth."

"Maybe, but it's a natural reaction. With teeth like yours, anyone who takes chances can lose a leg."

"But how do I show him I'm friendly?"

Morris shrugged, and turned the fish head over. "I've never had the problem," he said. "As far as I'm concerned, people are just a source of food. Stick around them long enough, and they're bound to throw away something you can eat." He examined an empty eye socket, and went on, "Most animals are afraid of them, but they've never given me much trouble."

"What's there to be afraid of?" Kilroy asked. "What do they do?"

"Kill, mostly," Morris replied. "Some of them kill for food, but there are others who seem to kill just for the fun of it. That's what makes them hard to understand."

"Odd," said Kilroy.

"Unless you're the one they decide to kill. Then it can be a lot worse than odd. They've got some pretty unpleasant methods of killing."

Kilroy thought for a moment. "I remember once we saw a ship," he said. "It had stopped, and it had a dead sperm whale alongside. They were stripping the blubber off. But I don't know how they killed it, so I don't know if it was unpleasant or not."

"It was," said Morris, peering into the gaping fish mouth. "They fired a big dart into it, which exploded under the skin."

"Well, we didn't see that part of it. We just saw them taking the blubber."

"What did you do?"

"Went in and ate what we could. You don't get a chance like that every day."

"You're right there. Some days, I feel as though I could take care of a whole whale, all by myself."

"There's a funny thing about people," Kilroy went on. "Just when you think you've got them figured out, they do something you don't expect. Up to the north, where they live in little skin huts, they treat an orca like a god. They sing songs to him, carve images of him— nothing's too good for an orca."

"They sound like nice people," Morris observed. "How do they feel about gulls?"

"I never heard. But then, just a little further south, something happened that was exactly the opposite."

"What was that?"

"We were going along the shores of this bay, and up on the cliffs there were two men who'd been cutting trees. They'd strip the trees, cut them into long logs, then slide them down a chute into the water. Just as we went past the chute one of these men took careful aim, then cut loose with a log that came zooming down, shot across the water, and hit my Aunt Millicent right in the kidneys. You could tell it was deliberate, because this man jumped up and down and cheered as though he'd done something great."

"I've known people like that. What happened?"

"We waited around till evening, when these two men got in their boat to go home. They had to cross the bay, and when they were about half-way across we came up and flipped their boat over."

"And?"

Kilroy grinned. "One man made it to shore. The one who'd aimed the log didn't."

"Served him right. How was your aunt?"

"Her back gives her trouble in cold weather, otherwise she's all right. It gives her something to talk about."

"I guess she's lucky. Some lout shot an arrow at me once, but he missed."

"Why would he want to do that?"

"Who knows? Any more than the clown who—" Morris closed his eyes, and ruffled his feathers— "I can't talk about it. Every time I think of it I get so mad I can't see straight."

"Tell me about it, maybe it'll make you feel better."

Morris took a deep breath. "There's this restaurant in town, down on the waterfront. It's got a big deck out over the water, so people can pretend they're eating on a ship. It's a good place to go for scraps, because they're always throwing things over the side. For some reason, it amuses them to watch us eat."

"I guess some people are easily amused," said Kilroy.

"Not this one. Nothing so simple as just watching us eat."

"What did he do?"

"He was having steamed clams. He'd strip the skin off the neck of each clam and throw it over the side, until he had a lot of us circling around waiting for the next bit. Then he took two clams—" Morris closed his eyes again, controlling himself with difficulty— "tied them together with a long piece of string, and threw them into the water. Among the crowd of us was a gull

21

named Lester, whom I've never really liked, and Lester swooped down and got one clam, swallowed it, and began to take off. I got the other clam—without seeing they were tied together—and swallowed it, and all of a sudden I found myself being dragged through the water, as Lester struggled to get airborne. I was yelling, and Lester was yelling, and neither of us knew quite what had gone wrong. It was hell."

"How did it end?"

"Well, Lester had got his clam farther down than I had, so I had to cough mine up. Lester flew off with my clam trailing out behind him, and a lot of other gulls went in and made passes at it. I think one of them finally got it off the string."

Kilroy thought about this for a while. "If I could talk to people," he said, at last, "I could find out what makes them do these things. I have a feeling they may be more intelligent than they seem, but there's no way to be sure until I can talk with them."

"Well, good luck," said Morris. "I don't care how bright they are, just so long as they keep the food coming."

"I thought I could talk with this man, here, because he's been copying my voice. But it makes it harder if he's afraid of my teeth."

"Keep your mouth closed," Morris suggested. "Try going at him with a tight-lipped smile."

"No," said Kilroy. "It's fear in general that spoils it. If I could get him over that, the rest should be easy." He thought a moment, then said, "What *is* fear, any-way?"

22

Morris looked at him. "Are you serious?" he said. "You don't know what it is?"

"No."

"Fear is—well—" Morris looked at the fish head, then back at Kilroy— "it's being afraid for your life."

"I don't get it," said Kilroy. "Tell me without using the word fear or afraid."

Morris cleared his throat. "It's thinking that something's about to kill you."

Kilroy considered this. "Like what?"

"Anything. A man—a dog—a—"

"A dog? Are you kidding?"

"Certainly not. Dogs love to try to catch gulls."

"Any dog came after *me* would regret it in a hurry."

"What about a shark, then? Or a whale?"

"Poof. We eat them all the time."

"Then a man."

"Men don't give us any grief. Except that one logger, and we fixed him."

"Don't you have any enemies?"

"None I can think of. I may have insulted someone without knowing it, but there's nobody I'm afraid of."

"All I can say is you're lucky."

"I don't call it lucky to be cooped up in this pool with nobody to talk to."

Morris eyed him coldly. "Well, I like *that*," he said.

"I didn't mean you," Kilroy added, quickly. "I meant I'd like to get through to that man. Or any man. If they're as smart as they think they are, they ought to be worth talking to."

"That's going to have to be your problem," Morris

said. "I've got to go look for food."

"I'll save you some next feeding time," said Kilroy, hoping he hadn't offended Morris. "If there's anything special you want, just let me know."

"So long as I can get it down, it's good," said Morris, spreading his wings. "Just no rubber boots or tennis balls. Or, come to think of it, those plastic beer-can holders. They're murder." With that he took off, and in a few moments was out of sight.

Kilroy wondered what it would be like to fly, and wished briefly he could be a gull, but then he thought of all the things that seagulls had to fear, and decided he was glad to be exactly what he was.

III

"I had the strangest dream last night," Morris said, the following day. "I dreamed I was trying to swallow a sardine, but it turned into a herring, then into an eel, then into a piece of rope, and then into you. I never did get it down."

"Thinking about your clam on a string, probably," said Kilroy.

"Do orcas ever dream?"

"Oh, yes. I keep dreaming I'm back in the pod."

"Doing anything special?"

"Well, last night I dreamed we were flying. I must say it was fun."

Morris thought about this. "I wouldn't exactly call it fun," he said. "You're up there for a purpose, either to get away from something or to look for something. My idea of fun would be to sit on the sand in the sun, and have someone feed me fish."

"You'd be sick of it before the day was out," Kilroy told him. "And believe me, I know. I don't even get to do tricks, like old Laughing Boy over there."

They looked at the dolphin, who was performing a series of tricks for his trainer, being rewarded with a fish every time he completed one. "I guess it takes all kinds to make a world," Morris observed. "To me, that's about as interesting as watching a chicken lay eggs. What's the big deal?"

"It's no big deal, but it's something to do. What irritates me is that he gets paid for doing it."

"Why not do the same tricks, to show them how easy it is?" Morris suggested. "If the man knew there was nothing to it, he might not give him the fish." ·

"All right," said Kilroy. "What have I got to lose?" The dolphin was jumping through a hoop, and while there was nothing for Kilroy to go through he made the same kind of jump, only higher. But the man was so busy with the dolphin he didn't see Kilroy, and the leap went unnoticed.

"I've an idea," Morris said when, for the third time, Kilroy's trick was ignored. "Let me stand on your head, and we'll go down there and get his attention."

"The dolphin won't like it," said Kilroy. "He wants that end of the pool to himself."

"If the dolphin doesn't like it he can go somewhere else," Morris replied. "I'll teach him to fly, and he can buzz off to Miami."

With that Morris hopped onto Kilroy's head, and Kilroy started a fast tour of the pool, barely avoiding the dolphin as he charged past. Morris, his wings outstretched for balance, made caterwauling noises of delight.

"Hey!" the dolphin shouted. "What do you think you're doing?"

"We're off to see the wizard!" Morris called back, over his shoulder. "Stay out of the way if you don't want to be sunk! Full speed ahead! Women and children man the lifeboats! Once more unto the breach, dear friend, and this time let's show them what speed really is!"

Kilroy made another circuit, creating a bow wave that swamped the gutters and made the pool seem to rock, and then, back at his end, he rose upright in the water, while Morris scrambled onto his nose and posed like the eagle atop a flagpole. Then Kilroy sank back and Morris jumped to the poolside, while the trainer stared in open-mouthed disbelief and the dolphin screamed in outrage.

"That was good," Kilroy said, to Morris. "I haven't had so much fun in a long time."

"Let's see what effect it had," Morris replied. "I don't know how he can give that dolphin a fish now."

The trainer stood, a fish in one hand and the hoop in the other, still staring at Kilroy. Then, on an impulse, he threw the fish across the pool, and Kilroy rose from the water and caught it.

"Well, thanks for sharing," Morris said, as Kilroy swallowed the fish. "I'm certainly glad I gave *you* the idea."

"I'm sorry," Kilroy replied. "I wasn't thinking."

"Oh, that's all right." Morris' voice was breezy and offhand. "I'm used to having to scrounge for my food."

"Wait a minute," said Kilroy, and he swam across the pool and put his head out of water at the trainer's feet. Then he opened his mouth in a toothy smile and began to bob up and down, higher each time, until he was almost tail-walking.

"That's my act!" the dolphin shrieked. "You're stealing my business!"

"It's a free country," Kilroy replied, still smiling. "Anyone can do tricks who wants to."

The trainer, not sure that Kilroy wasn't going to come right out of the pool, reached hurriedly into the bucket and produced another fish, which he flipped to Kilroy over the dolphin's noisy protests. Kilroy took the fish in his teeth, turned and crossed the pool in two leaps, and presented the prize to Morris.

"That's more like it," Morris said, swallowing the fish in one gulp. "See if you can spring him loose from another."

"Robbers! Thieves! Footpads!" the dolphin shouted. "First you steal my business, and then you steal my fish!"

The trainer was astonished at the sight of an orca giving his food to a gull, and to see if it would happen again he threw another fish to Kilroy, who caught it and flipped it to the dolphin. "Here, boy," Kilroy said. "Your need seems to be greater than mine."

The dolphin snatched the fish out of the air. "Don't think you're doing *me* a favor," he said. "It was mine in the first place."

Later, back in the aquarium office, the trainer was talking with the man who'd made recordings of Kilroy's voice.

"That's an unusual orca we've got there," he said, rinsing out the empty fish bucket.

"What's unusual about him?" the recording man asked. "Other than that he tried to take my arm off."

"He does tricks just for the fun of it," the trainer replied. "I gave him a fish, and he gave it away. Twice."

"Maybe he isn't hungry. Maybe he only wants to eat people."

"He could have had my leg if he'd wanted it. He just likes to do tricks."

"Well, it was no trick when he came after me. His teeth looked as big as cavalry sabres."

"Maybe you annoyed him. How do you know what was on those recordings?"

"It was his own voice. How could he get annoyed at that?"

"It depends on what he was saying. Maybe he'd been cursing you out, and when you played it back he thought you were cursing him."

"Well, if you want to play with him, feel free. I don't intend to be orca bait just to prove a minor point."

"Look at it this way—if he *really* does tricks for the fun of it, then there's nothing we can't teach him. We can get him to dance, and sing—"

"Get a grip on yourself, pal. The orca wasn't born who ever sang."

"Don't be so sure. They like music, so there's no reason they shouldn't imitate it."

"So you get him to sing. Then what?"

"Think what these Marinelands would pay for an orca like that! Even if he doesn't sing, he's worth a lot of money for his tricks. Build up a big repertory for him, and he'll be worth a million." The recording man looked at him with scorn, and he added, "Well—several thousand."

"If you want to try it, go ahead," the other replied. "But if you want my opinion, you're risking an arm or a leg for a few lousy thousand dollars."

"Since when did you get to sneer at a few thousand dollars?"

"Ever since I looked at the cost of artificial limbs."

The trainer gazed out the window. "I think we've got something here," he said. "I think we should make the most of it."

So he set about teaching Kilroy a whole set of tricks. As soon as Kilroy understood what was wanted he did it immediately, and all the time he was trying to think of some way he could talk to the trainer. He clicked and he whistled and he honked, and he tried to make noises like those the trainer made, but nothing came out quite right and it was clear he wasn't getting through. The trainer was interested only in the tricks as such, and Kilroy was interested in the tricks as a way of getting to talk, and since they were working at cross purposes the only progress they made was with the tricks. Kilroy did everything: he jumped over a bar and through a burning hoop; he butted balls with his nose and balanced plates on his head; he rushed around the pool with a monkey dressed as a jockey riding his back (Morris tried to ride his head, but the trainer kept shooing him off with a long stick); and, in short, he did practically everything except sing. The trainer played records for him, and while he listened to them intently he wasn't moved to sing, partly because they weren't real music and partly because he was more interested in how they worked than in what they were playing.

Here was the same sort of device that had made a copy of his voice, and he felt that if he could somehow turn it around he could say something the trainer would understand, but it was the turning around that had him stumped. No matter how hard he tried to reason it out, he came up against a blank wall. It got so that he was doing the tricks just for the exercise, while he let his mind explore the problem.

The dolphin went into a black sulk, and refused to speak to anyone. He finally had to be transferred to another tank, where he wouldn't see Kilroy performing. As he was lifted up in the sling he looked down at Kilroy and said, "I hope you know what's in store for you."

"What?" said Kilroy, happy to be seeing the last of him.

"You'll have fame and you'll be admired," the dolphin said, as though reading an omen in the sky. "But it will all be hollow. It will be as ashes in your mouth. People will come for miles to see you and then they will go away, leaving you alone with your poor, pitiful bag of tricks. There's more to life. than just jumping through a hoop, but you'll never know it. You'll end your days in an old actors' home, boring others with your newspaper clippings and your stories of bygone triumphs. I feel sorry for you."

"You didn't sound so sorry when I was doing the tricks," Kilroy observed. "You sounded just plain jealous."

"There isn't a jealous bone in my body," the dolphin replied. "It was only that it hurt me to see you selling your soul so cheaply."

At this Morris became convulsed with laughter, and he sat in the gutter and made a sound exactly like the braying of a donkey. He kept it up until the dolphin was out of sight, and then he hopped on Kilroy's head and clucked as though to a horse while Kilroy dashed around the pool. Morris maintained his perch even when Kilroy executed a few leaps, and the aquarium workmen stopped what they were doing and gathered around to watch. The show lasted for perhaps fifteen minutes, and at the end the workmen applauded. The trainer, who'd watched the whole thing from his window, smiled.

"A gold mine," he said, to nobody in particular. "A guaranteed, eighteen-karat gold mine."

One day, when Kilroy and Morris had done every trick they knew, they retired to a corner of the pool to catch their breaths and see if they couldn't think of something new. They found that even the most elaborate trick became dull if it was repeated often enough, and they were sure that between them they could come up with something that would add a little zest to their routine.

"Here's an idea," said Morris. "Suppose we reverse our roles. You teach me to swim, and I—"

"And you teach me to fly?" Kilroy put in. "Are you out of your mind?"

"It just came off the top of my head," said Morris. "There are a few bugs would have to be worked out."

"I'll say there are. Besides, you already know how to swim."

"That isn't swimming, that's just paddling. I'd like

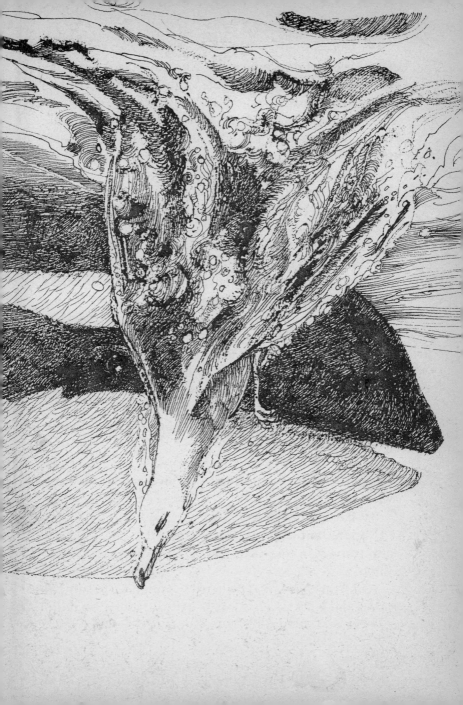

to zoom around underwater the way you do."

"There's no trick to that," Kilroy told him. "Just hold your breath, and zoom."

"Let's see if I can do it." Morris took a deep breath, then held it and put his head under the water. He flapped his wings and kicked his feet, but his tail remained above the surface like a small, feathered buoy. Finally, spluttering and gasping, he brought his head up. "No go," he said. "I'm doing something wrong."

"Well, you dive into the water for fish," Kilroy said. "Why not take a high dive, and just keep on going?"

"I'll try anything once," said Morris, and he took off and rose above the pool. He circled for a moment, then folded his wings and dropped like a stone, hitting the water with a resounding splash. He thrashed around beneath the surface for a few moments, then came up and shook his head to clear it. Spray flew in all directions, and his voice when he spoke sounded clogged. "I'm still doing something wrong," he said. "I don't swim, I just flounder."

"It takes a while," Kilroy told him. "Nobody can be perfect the first time."

"I saw an interesting thing when I was up there, though," Morris said. "There's a big truck headed this way."

"What kind of truck?" Kilroy asked.

"I don't know. It was just coming through the gate, and turning in this direction. Then I dove, and everything went black."

As he finished speaking a truck pulled up beside the pool, and Kilroy saw it was fitted with a derrick and a

34

large sling. It was the same kind of truck that had brought him from the airport, and for a moment he had a wild surge of hope that it might be going to take him to the ocean. But then his instinct told him this was impossible; men didn't go to all the trouble they had had with him, just to return him to his home waters. He was being shipped someplace else, and as the sling was lowered into the water he had a wild desire to flee, and to hide where they couldn't find him. But there was no hiding place in the pool, and when the men jumped in and brought the sling toward him he lay still, and let them strap him into it.

"Where are you going?" Morris called, circling above the pool. "What are they going to do with you?"

"I have no idea," Kilroy replied. "I'll just have to wait and see."

"They can't do this!" Morris squawked. "I won't let them!" He peeled off and dove at the nearest man, who flinched away from Morris' beak and then struck back at him. Morris climbed steeply, and came around for another dive.

"Don't waste your time," Kilroy told him. "You'll just get yourself hurt, and it won't do any good."

"I don't want you to go!" Morris replied, shrilly. "The place won't be the same without you!"

"I don't want to go, either," said Kilroy. "But I don't seem to have much choice."

"You might at least put up a fight! Thrash a little! Bite them! You could snap that nearest one in half without even trying!"

"It'd only make things worse. If they want me to go

somewhere, I've got to go." Slowly, Kilroy and the dripping sling were lifted from the water, and guided toward the truck.

"What am I going to do for fun?" Morris wailed. "I never knew what fun was until you came here!"

"I've liked it, too," said Kilroy. "Believe me, this isn't my idea."

"I'd believe you if you put up even a little fight," said Morris. "I don't think you care."

"I *do* care," Kilroy replied, as the sling was lowered gently into the truck. "I'm going to miss you. But—" The rest of his sentence was lost as the men wrapped him in wet blankets, and the driver put the truck in gear. The truck lumbered away from the pool and Morris followed it for a while, calling to Kilroy, but when he got no answer he finally veered away and flew into the town, where he knocked the cover off a garbage can and strewed refuse all over the sidewalk. Then he chased a cat up a tree and dive-bombed a policeman, and as a final gesture of vengeance he dropped clamshells on a garden party. A headline in the local paper next day read: "Mad Gull Wreaks Havoc; Socialites Bombarded."

IV

After a long trip, by truck and airplane and then by truck again, Kilroy arrived at his new home. The aquarium was larger than the first one, and there were tiers of seats on both sides of the main pool, seats that he found out later were occupied by tourists who came to watch the show. His pool was off the main one, and had a large wall, or fence, separating it from the sea, so his water was constantly changed by the tides and was always fresh. His first thought was to see if he could jump over the fence, but it had been made too high for that, and after exploring all the possibilities he gave up and resigned himself to captivity. It was tantalizing to be so close to the sea without being able to swim away, but at least it was better than being cooped up in one small pool. If Kilroy had learned anything in the last little while, it was to make the best of what was at hand and not try to do the impossible.

There was a sort of sluice gate leading from his pool into the main one, and this was opened when the people wanted him to go from one to the other. The first time he went into the main pool he saw, at the opposite end, three bottlenosed dolphins who were regarding him in silence. "Oh, no," he said, to himself. "Not *that* again!" He looked at the dolphins, and they looked at him, and he finally decided to see if he could start things off on a friendly basis. He went slowly toward them, and they clustered together and waited.

"My name is Kilroy," he said.

The dolphins didn't answer.

"If we're going to share the same pool we might as well try to get along," he went on. "As far as I'm concerned, we're all in one family."

There was a short silence, then one of the dolphins said, "I'm glad to hear it. Where'd you come from?"

"Another aquarium."

"Then you're not a dolphin eater?"

"No, and I never have been. Our pod never once touched a dolphin." This wasn't exactly the truth, but it was close enough because he himself had never eaten one.

"I thought you said you came from an aquarium," the dolphin said.

"I did, but before that I lived in the ocean. I was born in the ocean."

"Then how come you've never eaten dolphin?"

"Look," said Kilroy. "If you'll just stop being suspicious, we can all have a good time. At this other aquarium there was a dolphin who made life miserable for both of us, just because he'd had an uncle who was eaten by orcas. Forget what other orcas have done, and listen to me when I say I want to be friendly. What have you got to lose?"

The dolphins looked at each other, and then the

first one said, "Come to think of it, I guess you're right. If you want to be friendly, there's no reason we shouldn't be."

"All right, then. My name is Kilroy. What are yours?"

"I'm called Groucho," said the first.

"I'm Harpo," said the one on his left.

"Chico," said the third.

"Glad to know you," said Kilroy. "You sound Italian. Are you?"

"Don't ask me," Groucho replied. "The trainer gave us our names."

"What's he like?" Kilroy asked.

"He's all right. He doesn't work us too hard."

"Can you talk to him?"

Groucho thought for a moment, then said, "Not really. You know what he wants by the signals he gives you, but that isn't exactly talking."

"I think there's got to be some way to get through to people," Kilroy said. "I have a feeling they may be a lot more intelligent than we think they are."

"I'll tell you one thing about this man," Chico put in. "He gives you a fish only when you do the trick right. You can't cut corners with him."

"I don't care about the fish," Kilroy replied. "I'd like to know what he's thinking."

"That never occurred to me," said Groucho. "To me, he's just another way of getting food."

Harpo, who had drifted slightly away from the others, now started a series of leaps, going high in the air and then falling back only to shoot straight up again, like a bouncing ball. Each leap was more frenzied than

39

the first, until it looked as though he were trying to fly.

"That means the trainer's coming," Groucho observed. "Harpo always goes a little crazy when training time begins."

"Why?" said Kilroy. "Doesn't he get enough exercise?"

"He likes to get the first fish. I think he's afraid the bucket'll be empty before he's had his share."

The trainer flipped a fish to Harpo, who swallowed it and, grinning, rejoined the others.

"All right," Groucho said. "Places for Act One." Chico and Harpo fell in line behind him, and all three waited for the signal from the trainer.

"Where do I go?" Kilroy asked.

"Wait till he tells you," Groucho replied. "I don't know where you fit into the act."

The trainer blew a whistle and the three dolphins started off, leaping in unison as they made a circuit of the pool. Then they gathered beneath him and put their heads out of water, and he tossed a fish to each one. Kilroy, who was afraid he was being left out of the act, also put his head out of water, smiling broadly to attract the trainer's attention.

"Oh, you want one, too?" said the trainer, and he tossed a fish to Kilroy, who held it in his teeth, then took it back and laid it at the trainer's feet. The man stared at him, then said, "What's the matter with it?" and picked up the fish and examined it.

"We haven't finished our act yet," Groucho said. "Why don't you wait until—" But Kilroy was off on a tour of the pool, leaping as the dolphins had done, and ending back in front of the trainer. Again the man gave him a fish, and again Kilroy gave it back. "Believe me, I don't mean to sound impatient," Groucho said, "but maybe if we finish our act first, then he'll know where to fit you in."

"I'm sorry," Kilroy said, backing away. "I just wanted to make a point." He retired across the pool and the dolphins waited for the signal for their next trick, but the trainer kept looking at Kilroy, trying to understand what was going on. Finally Harpo started leaping straight up in the air, and the trainer returned his attention to the dolphins. They went through a whole series of tricks, jumping through and over various obstacles, but the trainer was so distracted that at one point he forgot to give them their fish, and Harpo had to start leaping again to remind him.

When, finally, the training session was over, Groucho came to Kilroy and, trying as hard as he could to be tactful, said, "I hope you didn't think I was rude, asking you to wait for us to finish."

"Not in the least," Kilroy replied. "It was my fault entirely."

"This morning it didn't matter," Groucho went on, "because it was only a rehearsal, but if it had been show time it would have disrupted the act."

"When is the show?" Kilroy asked.

"We do two a day, in the afternoons," Groucho told him. "Then on weekends we do three, one morning and two afternoon. It comes out to sixteen shows a week."

"That's a lot of shows," Kilroy observed. "I should think you'd be good and sick of it by now."

Groucho looked at the other two, who were chasing

41

each other around the perimeter of the pool. "I suppose if we thought about it, we would be," he replied. "But it's exercise, and we get food for it, so we can't complain."

"What I'd like to do is talk to the trainer," Kilroy said. "If I could just do that, I have a feeling life wouldn't be so dull."

"You don't want much, do you?" said Groucho.

"I don't know. It may be perfectly simple, once I find the key."

"Well, let me know how you make out," Groucho replied. "So long as he keeps the fish coming, I don't care what he has to say." And with that he swam off and joined the others.

Somewhat to the dolphins' annoyance a new training schedule was started, in which Kilroy had a leading part. The trainer, seeing that Kilroy was doing the tricks for their own sake rather than for food, reasoned there was nothing he wouldn't do if he just got the idea, and to this end he began to devise all sorts of elaborate routines. The trouble was that they were all variants of the same trick: Kilroy would butt a ball, or jump a hurdle, or smack the water so many times with his tail, and the only really tricky things were the props the trainer invented to go along with the basics. He made, for instance, a large fountain pen, which Kilroy grasped in his mouth in an act during which he was supposed to sign a contract; the same stick that was the core of the pen could also be made into a baseball bat, when the story accompanying the act was changed. Or, a flag, for the Iwo Jima monument. Or a toothbrush, for a domestic scene. And so on. In short, Kilroy was doing one basic trick, the extremely simple one of holding something in his mouth, while the trainer invented the frills that went with it.

To Kilroy this was deeply discouraging, and he finally decided to invent a trick of his own, one that would show he was thinking instead of merely obeying orders. He pondered the problem for a while, and then, during a training session when he was supposed to leap high in the air and butt a ball with his nose, he made the leap, flipped over and slapped the ball with his tail, and returned to the water in a grotesque parody of a swan dive.

"No, no, no!" the trainer shouted. "Hit it with your nose! Your nose!" Kilroy didn't understand the words but he got the message, and he glumly circled the pool, shot in the air, and hit the ball with his nose as he was supposed to. "Marvellous!" the trainer cried. "Perfect! Bravo!" Kilroy sank to the bottom of the pool, and sulked. I'd like to teach this man a trick or two, he thought. I'd like to have him swallow a salmon in one bite, or find a squid down where the water's as black as midnight, or leap his full length out of the water, or—or—I'd like to teach him to *think*. That would be something. I'd gladly put up with all this silliness, just to know that he was thinking. We might even have some thoughts in common, and we could exchange ideas and teach one another things we hadn't known before. The thought of sharing ideas with a man was so exciting that Kilroy came up from the bottom, opened his mouth wide, and wiggled his tongue at the trainer. The gesture reminded him of

Morris, who had tweaked his tongue the first time they met, and he did it on the chance it might mean something to the trainer beyond the simple gesture. The man looked at him, laughed, then reached into a bucket and threw him a fish. "Oh, all right," he said. "You've worked for it." Kilroy took the fish by the tail and then, with his head out of water, spun around faster and faster and finally let the fish go. It sailed out in a bright, twinkling arc, and landed in the grandstand seats. The trainer watched it, then cast a baleful glance at Kilroy. "That's gratitude for you," he said. "Now I've got to go clean it up." Kilroy made a honking noise through his blowhole, then started a series of fast laps around the pool, chasing an imaginary flying fish, until the trainer opened the sluice gate to his own pool and let him through.

Kilroy's first public show was a thundering success. The grandstand was filled with people in brightly colored shirts and dresses, and from them rose a gabble of voices punctuated by the shouts and cries of children; soft-drink and hot-dog vendors hawked their wares, and over the loudspeaker came a program of canned music that under other circumstances would have been offensive to Kilroy's sense of hearing. As it was, it was part of the circus atmosphere and as such exciting, and while Kilroy wasn't nervous he was so stimulated that he couldn't resist doing a few small jigging motions of his own. He was like a racehorse at the starting gate, waiting to be released to show what he could do.

The act started off with Kilroy and the three dolphins covering an obstacle course around the pool, and when the dolphins received their fish Kilroy stood by and applauded. Then they swam in formation, with the dolphins rotating from one side to the other of their large companion, and finally tail-walking ahead of him while he pretended to give chase. Then came Kilroy's solo act, in which he was rigged out in a Revolutionary hat and made to do a number of things that had an allegedly patriotic theme. All he was really doing was holding something in his mouth, and hitting the water with his tail, and all the simple, humdrum bits of routine, but the voice over the loudspeaker read all sorts of meanings into his acts. The audience applauded wildly, but to Kilroy the whole act was frustrating because he'd been drubbed into doing meaningless things when all the time he'd wanted to do something better. He did his act exactly as he was supposed to because every time he tried something a little different he got a warning scowl from the trainer, and he finally gave up and went through the mindless routine as quickly and as professionally as he could.

When, finally, the sluice gate was opened and he returned to his pool, the audience cheered and whistled and clapped, but the noise meant nothing to Kilroy other than a lot of people making sounds. He couldn't even hear them using a language, and he wondered briefly if he'd been performing for a group of subnormal specimens, incapable of thought or speech on their own. It was an explanation, but it was such a degrading one that he preferred not to think of it, telling himself instead that they were being taught a new language by watching him and the dolphins. If this were true, he thought, then perhaps he could have

45

a hand at teaching them. . . . He stopped, as the beauty of the idea came over him. Suppose he were chosen to teach people something—anything he wanted—what would he do? He decided he'd teach them the things they seemed to be missing, or misunderstanding, about life. He'd heard that people were cruel but he'd never seen them in an act of cruelty so he didn't know if they were or not. He'd heard they were wasteful of life, and if this was so there was a lot he could teach them, because orcas valued every life as worth something, to be surrendered only in the interest of food or the preservation of the group. No orca ever wasted a life and no orca ever killed for the sheer fun of it, as he'd heard humans did. There was nothing more wasteful or obscene than killing for fun, and if he could stop just one human from doing that he'd figure his time had been well spent.

He remembered the time, perhaps a year ago, when his pod had been in the Northwest, and an old bull orca had managed to run himself aground. He was past his prime, and it was time for another bull to assume leadership, and nobody could be exactly sure why this one had got himself in such a stupid situation. There was some thought he'd done it deliberately, to avoid the inevitable battle; others thought his eyesight was failing, or his sonar had begun to malfunction, and then he'd run aground accidentally while chasing a seal. Whatever the reason there he was, left high and dry by the receding tide, while the weight of his body, unsupported by water, began to press heavily on his lungs. He might have survived until the next high tide but he didn't seem to want to; he just gave up and lay there with his eyes closed, breathing heavily and bleeding from the spots where his drying skin had begun to crack. The rest of the pod circled in the deeper water, offering suggestions and advice and conferring among themselves as to what to do, but nothing availed and at the turn of the tide the old bull gasped three times and ceased breathing. Then a strange thing happened. A man, dressed in furs and skins, appeared in a skin-covered boat, took one look at the dead orca, and paddled away as fast as he could. Within a short time people began to appear along the shore, and they gathered around and performed a dance, stamping their feet and making gull-like cries, and this dance went on for what seemed like, to the other orcas, an unnecessarily long time. At last the people got down to the intelligent part of the routine, which was to take out their knives and dismember the carcass, and within a short while all that was left was a small pile of scraps for the dogs. The pod, under the leadership of the next senior bull, moved away, and when in a few months' time they revisited the spot they saw a large wooden pole, covered with carved figures, rising from the beach where the orca had died. The figures were hard to make out, but the topmost one had large teeth and a gaping grin, and was clearly a representation of an orca. Kilroy had thought about this, on and off, and he couldn't make out its meaning beyond the fact that it seemed like some sort of compliment, or gesture of respect. It was one of those mysteries about people he wanted to unravel, if only he could find the key to their nature.

In the meantime he did his tricks as the trainer

wanted, and tried to keep his mind from turning to jelly. People came from miles around to see the miraculous performing orca that could sign the Declaration of Independence and count the original colonies with slaps of his tail, and all the while Kilroy was saying to himself, "Grab the pen—give it back—slap the water —two-three-four-five—up in the air—hit the bell—I wish they'd get some fresh salmon for a change— six-seven-eight-nine—or a squid; I haven't had a decent piece of squid in months—around the tank— jump the hurdle—and the last time I ate an octopus— eleven-twelve-thirteen—is this the first show today, or the second?—salute the flag—I wonder what's got into Groucho; he hasn't spoken for three days—twice around the pool—once—twice—I guess he must be jealous—well, he's welcome to the act if he wants it— here comes the finale—up on the tail—smile nicely— open up that sluice gate, will you?—There. At last. Peace and quiet."

One afternoon, at the conclusion of the last show, he charged through the sluice gate to the cheers and applause of the audience, and heard an odd but somehow familiar noise in all the tumult. It was the braying of a seagull, and Kilroy looked back and saw, atop one of the light poles, his old friend Morris, beating his wings together and screeching, "Encore! Encore! Up the orca!"

"Morris!" Kilroy said, with delight. "What are you doing here?"

Morris glided down and lit at the edge of the pool. "I just thought I'd come and see how you're doing," he said.

"How did you find where I was?"

"If you ever want to know anything, ask the birds," Morris replied. "We don't do a lot of talking, but nothing escapes our attention. Given time, I could tell you what they had for dinner at the White House last night, or whose Chevrolet Impala was parked in the wrong driveway, or why there was a rash of sea-food poisoning at the Nosh-a-Fish Luncheonette. I could tell you—"

"O.K., O.K., I believe you," Kilroy cut in. "I just didn't expect to see you, that's all."

"We gulls move in strange and mysterious ways," said Morris. "We wheel on pinioned wings."

Kilroy looked at him. "Say that again."

"We wheel on pinioned wings. What's the matter with that?"

"It doesn't sound like you and besides, it's redundant. Pinions are wings."

Morris sighed. "That's another reason I wanted to leave," he said. "The old place isn't the same."

"What are you talking about?"

"Oh, some mystic joined the group," Morris said. "A seagull with a mission. He's got everybody talking like a revival meeting."

"Do you have to listen to him?"

"Ha. Just try not to. You're likely to be stoned."

"Well, I guess things are poor all over. I'd settle for a good revival meeting—whatever that may be—just to get a change of pace around here."

"They seem to keep you busy."

"If you want to call it busy. It's about as stimulating as counting plankton."

49

Morris thought for a moment, then said, "You're awfully good at it."

"Big deal," Kilroy replied. "I'd rather be on my own."

"Did you ever wonder what would happen if you weren't quite so good?"

"What do you mean?"

"Suppose you were to flub a trick or two. What would happen?"

"The trainer'd make me do them over and over until I got them right."

"But suppose you didn't want to do them right. What then?"

"I don't know. They're so simple it never occurred to me."

"Think about it. He can't *make* you do them. There's nothing in the world he can do to force you."

"He can withhold my food."

"Pooh. He's not going to starve you to death, just for a few tricks. The S.P.C.A.'d be on him like a ton of bricks."

"What's the S.P.C.A.?"

"Society for the Prevention of Cruelty to Animals. They got my grandfather out of a nasty jam once, when some kids caught him on a fishline and were flying him like a kite."

"You mean they have to have a society to keep people from being cruel?"

"They do indeed. And even they can't stop it all. You'd be amazed at what some people think is fun."

"I've never seen that side of them. Well, come to think of it, that logger was being deliberately cruel, but we fixed his hash. He wasn't cruel again."

"What I'm getting at is you're not going to suffer if you botch up a few tricks. And the worse you get, the more likely they are to want to get rid of you. People can't stand trained animals with minds of their own."

"It's a thought, all right. And it might be fun, just to see how the trainer reacts. I get the feeling he's a lot more interested in these tricks than I am."

"All right, then. What are you waiting for?"

Kilroy beamed, showing all his teeth. "Morris," he said, "don't ever leave me again. You make my life worth living."

"You were the one who left, not I," Morris reminded him. "And while you've got your mouth open, just hold it. You haven't had a decent cleaning job in weeks."

At the next show, when he was supposed to take the pen and sign the Declaration of Independence, Kilroy instead flipped the pen over his back, smacked it with his tail, and sent it spinning toward the seats. The hot-dog vendor saw it coming and managed to catch it, but in so doing spilled most of his hot dogs, and in a rage he flung the pen back at Kilroy, who took it in his teeth and raced once around the pool, while the trainer danced about and screamed, "No! No! No! Come back! Come back and do it right!" Grinning, Kilroy presented the pen to him, and when he leaned down to take it Kilroy squirted a big mouthful of water straight in his face. The audience, thinking this was part of the act, cheered and applauded, but the trainer came close to having a stroke. He tried to continue with the prepared act, following the script read by the announcer over the loudspeaker, but Kilroy did whatever appealed at the moment, adding new twists as they occurred to him. He found that no matter how many times he soaked the trainer it was always good for a laugh, and this led him to see what would happen if he soaked a few of the people as well. This brought screams along with the laughter, and there was a rush of people trying to get out of the front-row seats. One or two of the slower-moving people were stepped on, and although they had laughed the loudest when the trainer was drenched they no longer saw anything funny, and they raised their voices in shrill wails of protest. Finally, when panic and confusion had reduced the whole show to a shambles, the sluice gate was belatedly opened, and Kilroy glided gleefully into his own pool. Morris was waiting for him by the gate.

"Well, you did it," said Morris. "There's no question about that."

"It was fun," Kilroy replied. "I haven't had so much fun since I've been here."

"And you may not have again."

"Do you think they'll let me go?"

Morris hesitated. "That's just the trouble," he said. "You did it too well. They can't let you go, because you're too much of an attraction—even misbehaving the way you did, you had a certain repulsive appeal. The crowds love that."

"This was your idea, you know," Kilroy told him. "You were the one who said it would make them let me go."

"I know. I wasn't counting on your going quite so far overboard."

52

"So now what do I do?"

"If you ask me, your best move is to dog it. Don't do anything, and see what happens. Pretend you're sick—pretend you've gone deaf—pretend anything, but just don't do any more tricks."

"That won't be as much fun."

"No, but it may work better. The way you're going now, people will come from all over the country just to watch you misbehave. You're an asset, instead of a liability."

Kilroy shook his head. "I wish I could figure people out," he said. "The more unlikeable a thing is, the more they like it. They don't make sense."

"Don't try to figure them," Morris advised him. "That's a short-cut to insanity. Just do as I tell you, and maybe they'll let you go."

Kilroy sighed, emitting a large cloud of water vapor from his blowhole. "Things were never this complicated in the pod," he said. "All we had to worry about then was getting enough food."

"That's what happens when you get your food for free," Morris observed. "You buy a lot of other problems instead."

Slowly the sluice gate opened, and the trainer stood there, regarding Kilroy with hostile eyes. He'd changed his clothes since the show, but his hair was still wet. "All right, Mr. Smart Apple," he said. "Let's go back and start with the basics." Kilroy did nothing, and the trainer blew his whistle. "Move!" he commanded.

"Remember what I told you," Morris said, quietly. "Pretend you don't hear him."

Kilroy grinned broadly and rolled on his back, as though luxuriating in the sun. The trainer blew his whistle again, and Kilroy filled his mouth, rose from the water, and soaked the man to his socks. Then he drifted to the bottom of the pool, making small squeaking noises that echoed through the water. The trainer blew his whistle until he felt his lungs would burst, but Kilroy remained at the bottom of the pool, pretending to be looking for something.

Finally, at the end of a long and frustrating day, the trainer stamped into the office of the aquarium administrator. He was wet all over, water squilched in his shoes, and his eyes were bloodshot from salt water and rage. "That orca's had it," he announced. "I want nothing more to do with him."

The administrator, who'd been counting the day's gate receipts, looked up over his glasses. "What's the matter with him?" he asked, mildly.

"He's turned bad. There's no telling what he may do next. If you ask me, the safest thing would be to shoot him."

"That seems a little drastic," the administrator replied. "What's he done that's so bad?"

"He won't do any of his tricks. He's developed a mean streak. I wouldn't be surprised to see him leap out of the pool and snap up a child."

"Oh, come, now," said the administrator. "Aren't you being a little dramatic?"

"He went after the whole first row of spectators today. He deliberately started a panic. All he had to do was reach out and pluck up one of those squalling kids."

"But did he?"

"No. What I'm saying is he could have. And with this personality change, I can't guarantee what may happen."

"What personality change?"

"I've just been telling you—he's turned mean! He used to be all friendliness, and now he spits in my eye every time he gets a chance! He's anti-people! The only thing he'll let near him is that idiot seagull, and one of these days he's going to snap that bird right out of the air!"

"It seems to me," the administrator said, slowly, "that you're dreaming up a lot of problems just because you can't make him do your tricks."

"*I'm* dreaming up the problems?" the trainer shouted. "*I* am? Were you out there today? Did you see what he did?"

"No. I've been busy counting the money he's made."

"Well, you're going to need every nickel of it once he eats a child. There won't be enough money in the world to pay for the lawsuits."

"I think we'll worry about that when it happens. He's too valuable a property to let go."

"May the Lord preserve us all from idiots and administrators," the trainer intoned. "Will you do me just one favor?"

"What's that?"

"Will you remember that I was the one who said he should be shot?"

"I'll remember."

"And will you let me bring a rifle, in case he goes after the crowd?"

"Oh, I don't know about that. I'd rather have him bite someone than have you shoot someone by mistake."

"I'm not going to shoot anyone," the trainer said, his voice heavy with sarcasm. "I simply want a deterrent, in case this orca does what I think he may do."

"All right, then. But be careful."

"Don't worry. My middle name is Caution." And with that the trainer left the room, trailing little puddles of water behind him.

Every seat was sold for the next show. At the administrator's direction, the public-address system announced that the main act featured a wild killer whale, one that could not be trained, and the public was warned that their presence in the grandstands was at their own risk. Parents were advised to keep a firm hold on their children, and on no condition should anyone get close to the edge of the pool. As an added precaution a man would be standing by with a high-powered rifle, but the public could rest assured he would use it only as a last resort. With that the music rose to a crescendo, the sluice gate opened, and the trainer blew his whistle. Everyone strained forward, staring at the gate through which the monster would come. The tension probably hadn't been equalled since the days of ancient Rome, when the wild beasts were turned loose on the Christians.

For several seconds nothing happened, and once more the trainer blew his whistle. Still nothing.

"Fake!" shouted a voice in the bleachers.

Then there was a gasp from the crowd as a high, black dorsal fin appeared in the sluice gate, and they could see the monstrous body beneath. Kilroy glided into the main pool; the sluice gate closed behind him, and the trainer blew his whistle a third time. Kilroy sank to the bottom of the pool and stayed there, every now and then emitting tiny bubbles.

"He's resting now, ladies and gentlemen," the loudspeaker announced. "Gathering his strength for an assault. Any living thing that comes near him will be torn to shreds." As though making an offering to a god, the trainer threw a large salmon into the pool; it settled slowly to the bottom near Kilroy, but he ignored it. "Of course, that fish was not alive," the speaker went on. "The killer whale prefers the blood to be fresh. There's been a problem keeping him supplied with—ah—fresh meat, because his appetite is such that he could eat a whole flock of sheep, or one whole grain-fed steer, or—the like—in a very short time. He's known as the wolf of the sea, and with good reason. The werewolf of the sea would be better, because according to Eskimo legends the killer whale turns into a person, who sucks the blood of— He's moving now! He's coming to the surface! Everyone stand back, please!"

Slowly, Kilroy put his head above water, grinned, and rolled over on his back. Morris flew down from a light post, lit on Kilroy's chin, and began to clean his teeth.

"Keep it up," Morris said, in a low voice. "You're doing great."

58

"Fake!" shouted the same voice as before. "He's been drugged!"

"Ladies and gentlemen, this animal has not been drugged," the announcer said, a frantic tone creeping into his voice. "He's merely resting. There's no telling when he may . . ." The sentence trailed off, as Kilroy sank quietly to the bottom of the pool, leaving Morris swimming on the surface. Morris paddled about in a circle, rose and flapped his wings, then extended his neck and gave his imitation of a braying donkey. The audience applauded.

"Let's hear it for the trained seagull!" someone called. "At last we get some action!" There was laughter and applause, and the announcer, forgetting to cover his microphone, said, "Someone get that bloody bird outa there!" This brought more laughter, and cheers for Morris as he nimbly avoided the long-handled net the trainer stabbed at him. The trainer was in such a rage that he kept flailing away with the net, and he didn't return to his senses until a voice shouted, "Three strikes and you're out! Bring on the next batter!" Then he subsided, panting and glowering, while Morris cruised serenely about the center of the pool. For a moment the trainer was tempted to use his rifle, but he couldn't shoot at Morris without risking a ricochet into the crowd, so he could do nothing but accept defeat, while the spectators cheered and stamped and whistled.

Finally, in desperation, another gate was opened, and the three dolphins were let into the pool. They performed their tricks with neat precision, aware that they were regaining some of the prestige they'd lost to

Kilroy, and while they presented a pretty picture they didn't satisfy the crowd, which had come to see the mad killer whale. The dolphins leaped and pirouetted and tail-walked, and all the while the spectators stamped and clapped and chanted, "We want the killer whale! We want the killer whale!" At the conclusion of one leap, Groucho went down past Kilroy and said, "What's the matter? You sick, or something?"

"Just resting," Kilroy replied, cheerfully, and closed his eyes.

"I don't suppose you ever heard the saying that the show must go on."

"Never. What's it mean?"

"Let it pass." Groucho shot to the surface, tail-walked across the pool, and leaped through a hoop, while the audience continued its chant.

Finally, at the end of the day, the trainer went into the office of the administrator. "I've had it," he announced. "Either that orca goes, or I do. You can take your choice."

"Let's not go overboard about this," the administrator replied. "He didn't hurt anyone, did he?"

"That depends on what you mean by hurt. I can tell you, my nerves won't take another day like this. I'll be a raving maniac by sundown."

"He made a lot of money."

"And I wind up fanning a seagull with a fish-net. No, thank you. I know when I've had enough."

The administrator turned his chair, and looked out the window. "I'll be sorry to see you go," he said.

There was a long silence, while the trainer opened and closed his mouth like a fish out of water. Then he snapped his mouth shut, and stamped out of the room.

Kilroy's popularity lasted just about a week. A new trainer was brought in, but he had no better luck than the first, and after a while the word got around that the orca was sick, possibly having been starved in an attempt to make him fierce. The S.P.C.A. sent an agent around to investigate but he found nothing wrong; the orca was simply lethargic, and that was all there was to it. Attendance began to drop off, and the administrator found he was paying a great deal more to feed Kilroy than he was taking in at the gate, and the longer Kilroy stayed around the bigger he grew and the more he ate. Finally, after a week during which almost nobody came to the show, the administrator put through a call to the aquarium from which Kilroy had originally come.

"That orca you sold me," he announced, to the man at the other end of the line. "He's a dud. I want my money back."

"What do you mean, he's a dud?" came the reply. "There was nothing the matter with him when he left here."

"Well, there's something the matter with him now. He just lies at the bottom of the pool and sulks."

"I'm sorry, pal, but that's your problem. You must be doing something wrong."

"I'm not doing anything wrong! I even got a new trainer!"

"Well, that's show biz for you. You win a few, you lose a few."

"Will you refund half what I paid?"

"I won't refund a nickel. He was A-1 when he left here, and that's the end of my responsibility. Now, if you'll excuse me, I have work to do." The line went dead, and the administrator slowly replaced the instrument in its cradle. He looked out the window for a while, then went outside, where the new trainer was putting the dolphins through their paces.

"How's the orca?" the administrator asked.

"About the same," replied the trainer. "I think he's sick."

"The last thing we need is a lot of vet's bills," the administrator said. "Maybe you'd better turn him loose."

"Whatever you say. He's certainly no good to us the way he is."

"O.K., then, let him go." The administrator returned to his office, and the trainer went to Kilroy's pool and unlocked a section of the barrier that led to the sea. Morris, who was perched at the side of the pool, saw what was happening.

"Hey!" he squawked. "Kilroy! Look here!"

Kilroy had been prowling around the bottom of the pool, and he came to the surface and looked around. "What?" he said. "Where?"

"There! He's opening the gate!"

They both watched, hardly daring to believe their eyes, while the trainer swung the gate open. Then the trainer turned to Kilroy.

"O.K., sport," he said. "You're on your own. Good luck."

Kilroy cleared the gate in one giant leap and headed out to sea, leaping like a kangaroo, while Morris flew noisily overhead. The trainer watched them go, then swung the gate closed.

"For a sick orca, he sure recovered fast," he remarked, and bolted the gate and returned to the dolphins.

V

When they'd gone far enough to feel safe from pursuit, Kilroy stopped leaping and swam slowly, allowing Morris to ride on his head.

"What are you going to do?" Morris asked him.

"The first thing is get a good meal," Kilroy replied. "After that, I'm going to look for the pod."

"How do you know where they are?"

"I don't. I'll just play it by memory, and try to go where they usually are this time of year."

"That may take a long time." Morris was trying to say something, without putting it into so many words.

"I have all the time in the world," Kilroy told him. "I can hunt as I go, and sooner or later I'm bound to cross their path. If I don't, I can always join another pod."

"How do you hunt alone?" Morris asked. "I thought you always worked in groups."

"Well, it can't be too hard," Kilroy replied. "It's the same, except there aren't as many of you."

"I see," said Morris. "All right, then, go ahead. Remember to save some scraps for me."

Morris took off and spiralled upward, and Kilroy

flipped his tail in the air and headed down. The sea changed color as he sounded, from blue-green to bright blue, to darker blue, to midnight blue, and then to black, and all around him he heard the sounds of the deep—the snapping and crackling of millions of tiny shrimp, the grunts and groans and honks of other fish and marine animals, and from far away the high, squealing call of the baleen whale. Some of the sounds he recognized and some he didn't; he was in a world that was nothing but sounds, and he had neither the age nor the experience to sort them all out. Then he had to come up to breathe, and on the way devoured a few random fish, but he was still as hungry as though he'd eaten nothing. He broke the surface, and Morris came down and lit on the water near him.

"How'd you make out?" Morris asked.

"There wasn't much around," Kilroy replied. "Lots of little stuff, but nothing you'd really call a meal."

"Let's see your teeth." Kilroy opened his mouth, and Morris picked out a few scraps and then said, "I went up high to look around. I think I saw some tuna."

"Where?" said Kilroy, closing his mouth so fast he almost caught Morris' beak.

"Off on the horizon, to the northwest. They may not have been tuna, but they were doing one powerful lot of splashing."

"Maybe that's what I heard. There was something like splashing, but I couldn't figure it out."

"Do you want to go take a look?"

"I should say so. Lead the way."

Morris zoomed upward until he was just a speck in the sky, and then he headed on a straight course for the northwest, while Kilroy lunged along the surface. In a short while Kilroy could hear the individual sounds of the leaping fish, and he went below the surface and homed in on them at top speed, arriving in their midst almost before they knew what had struck. They scattered, but he managed to catch four big ones before they vanished, snapping each fish in half and then going for another one before stopping to eat. Then he devoured them at his leisure, and felt immeasurably better. He put his head out of the water, and opened his mouth for Morris.

"That's more like it," he said, as Morris began to clean his teeth.

"What you need is a scout," Morris replied. "Until you can hunt with a pod, you need someone to help you."

"Well, I'd never have found this meal without you," Kilroy said. "There's no getting around that."

"Then I'll be your scout," said Morris, happily. "I can fly out ahead, and tell you what's there. Who knows—I might even find your pod for you."

"That isn't much of a life for you," Kilroy replied. "Wouldn't you rather be with other birds?"

"If I need a bird, I can always find one," said Morris. "Besides, you told me never to leave you."

"Well, I appreciate it, but—"

"No buts about it. It's settled. Open wider."

Kilroy opened his mouth some more and Morris stepped inside, picking at the back teeth. "Tuna certainly are a greasy fish," he observed. "They've got more oil in them than a sperm whale."

"And believe me, after those dead salmon they

dished out at the aquarium, a few tuna are a treat," Kilroy said. "I could've eaten them all day."

"Well, they're pretty well scattered by now," Morris told him. "You'll never find them again."

Kilroy and Morris were so involved in their discussion that neither of them noticed the dorsal fin of a large shark which, attracted by the noise and the blood of Kilroy's foray against the tuna, was now coming to investigate. It moved slowly, propelled by lazy strokes of its tail, and it stopped a short distance away and examined the unlikely picture of the orca and the gull. Then it moved forward again, gaining speed, and opened its jagged, tooth-studded mouth. At the last minute Kilroy sensed its approach, but with Morris in his mouth he could neither dive nor turn to attack, so he did the only thing left: he leaped as high as he could from a standing start, spat Morris out of his mouth, and fell back into the water.

"Hey!" Morris shrieked, as he found himself propelled through the air in a cloud of feathers. "That's not funny!" He saw the shark rush past but could see no sign of Kilroy, who had apparently vanished straight down. The shark turned and circled back, undecided as to whether or not to pursue Kilroy into the depths. Its reasoning process was so elementary that once Kilroy was out of sight he was almost forgotten, and with no trail of blood to follow the shark rapidly began to lose interest. It surfaced and cast a baleful glance at Morris, who was flying in noisy, squalling circles to distract its attention, and then it cruised slowly about the area, looking for leftover scraps of tuna.

Morris had just begun to wonder how long Kilroy could stay down, when there was a sudden surge of water and a boil of foam, and Kilroy shot into the air, the shark gripped firmly in his jaws. There was a wild thrashing as the shark tried to reach Kilroy with its teeth, but the struggle was over almost as soon as it had begun, and in a matter of minutes Kilroy and Morris were having a feast. When, at last, they had eaten their fill, they set off once more for the northwest, moving slowly and contentedly.

"I must say, life with the gulls was never like this," Morris observed, from his perch atop Kilroy's head. "Those other birds don't know what they're missing."

"If someone had told me this morning we'd be doing this right now, I'd have said he was crazy," Kilroy replied. "I thought I was never going to get out of there."

"I told you they'd let you go," said Morris.

"Yes, but did you believe it?"

There was a pause. "Not really," said Morris. "I thought people were smarter than that."

"I guess we'll never know how smart they really are," Kilroy said. "But as far as I'm concerned it's not worth living in an aquarium to find out. That has got to be the dullest existence in the world."

"Some people keep birds in cages," Morris replied. "That must be even worse."

"Why do they do that?"

"Don't look at me. I just know what I've seen."

Kilroy shook his head. "There has to be a simple answer to them," he said. "But *I* sure can't figure it out. Almost everything they do is a contradiction: they kill animals, and keep them in cages, and then have a society that says they can't be cruel to them. They invent all sorts of machines, and then are amused by watching animals do stupid tricks. They get bored when something is good, and only like it when it turns bad. They—"

"Cut it out," Morris told him. "Next thing you know you'll find yourself going back, just to see if you can figure them out."

"*That*'ll be the day," said Kilroy. "That's one thing you need never worry about."

"Glad to hear it," said Morris. He looked at the western sky, which was turning pink. "Getting near my bedtime," he said. "Where do you want me to bunk?"

"Back along my fin would be best," Kilroy replied. "I'll try not to get your feet too wet."

"Well, it won't be the first time they've been wet," said Morris. "All I ask is some warning if you go all the way under."

"Right. I don't expect to, but you never can tell."

Morris moved to the high part of Kilroy's back, by his fin, and settled down to sleep. Kilroy swam slowly and evenly, and as night fell and the stars came out he felt a peace he'd never known. He hadn't felt this way before his capture because he didn't know anything different; now, with something to compare it to, he realized what peace and freedom really meant. Once or twice he almost found himself diving for the sheer pleasure of it, but just in time he remembered Morris, and maintained his even course. The night was calm, and the stars were reflected in the water, and it was a while before Kilroy realized that a subtle change had taken place in the sea. Animals and organisms that usually stayed in the depths rose to the surface at night, and the water was teeming with millions of different kinds of aquatic life. He sensed rather than saw a large mass ahead of him, and his instinct told him it was something to be attacked. With one flipper he splashed water on Morris to wake him, and when Morris shook his head and looked around, Kilroy said, in a low voice, "I'm going under. I won't be a minute."

"It better be important," Morris replied, and with that he hopped into the water, tucked his head under one wing, and went back to sleep.

Kilroy slipped beneath the surface and homed in on the mass, which was lying quietly about fifty yards ahead. He came at it from below, as he had with the shark, and as his teeth closed on it he knew his instinct had been right; he had attacked a massive squid, which had come up to hunt on the surface. Ten arms lined with suckers grasped at Kilroy's head and body, and a parrot-like beak snapped at him while inky fluid stained the water, but Kilroy's chomping jaws soon reduced the squid to bite-sized pieces, and he finished it off quickly. Remembering Morris, he took the tapered end of one arm to where the seagull, now wide awake, was riding on the water, and presented it to him.

"Here," he said. "Have a piece."

"Thanks," replied Morris, pecking at the morsel. "What is it?"

"Squid. Haven't you ever tried it?"

"Not this size. I raided a bait box once, but those were small ones." He picked up the piece, and began to swallow it. "It's like rubber," he said.

"Keep going," Kilroy told him. "You'll like it."

Morris kept swallowing, until finally the tip disappeared. "Well, thanks anyway," he said. "I appreciate the thought."

The rest of the night passed peacefully, then the stars faded and the sky turned first gray, then pink, and then red as the sun burst over the horizon. Morris woke, shook himself, and took off.

"I think I'll scout around a bit," he said, as he circled upward. "I've got to wear off those dreams."

"What dreams?" asked Kilroy.

"I guess it was the squid. I kept dreaming of snakes all night."

"I wouldn't know a snake from a cow," said Kilroy. "They're just names to me."

"Keep it that way," Morris replied, and flew off.

Kilroy went down a hundred feet or so and then came slowly to the surface, looking for breakfast. He ate a mackerel and a few small tuna but saw nothing really worthwhile, and when he came up to breathe he realized for the first time the problem of hunting alone. He'd been aware that it was easier with the pod, but he hadn't thought of the possibility that, working by himself, he might very possibly starve to death. He'd been lucky with the tuna, the shark, and the squid; now his luck seemed to be deserting him, and unless he could hunt with a pod again he was in deep trouble. Morris could help him spot food but Morris couldn't help him round it up, and the amount of food he needed was increasing every day. With this worry gnawing at the back of his mind he made another dive, this time down into the blackness, but the results were no better. As he came up, a school of small squid scattered at his approach and he got no more than a mouthful; he snapped up a couple of salmon without feeling he'd eaten anything, and as he neared the surface he lunged at a school of smelts that were less than satisfactory. He lay on the surface for a while, looking for Morris in the hope he might have discovered something, but the only birds he saw were a flight of Mother Carey's chickens, zipping low over the water and following the contours of the waves. He toyed briefly with the idea of trying to catch them, but he knew it would be impossible and besides, they were so small—the size of sparrows—that their value as food wouldn't be worth the energy expended. He made one more dive, this time one of desperation, and came up with nothing. Don't panic, he told himself. This is just a slack period; something's bound to show up before long.

He was resting on the surface when he saw Morris approaching from the northwest. Morris came down in a long glide, spreading his wing and tail feathers as brakes as he landed on the water in front of Kilroy's nose.

"What did you find?" Kilroy asked. "I'm starving."

"I didn't find much," Morris replied. "At any rate, much that would interest you. I've never seen the ocean so empty."

"Well, what *did* you find?" Kilroy persisted. "Anything interests me at this point."

"There's a pod of sperm whales several miles off," Morris told him. "One old bull, and some cows and younger ones. Maybe a dozen in all."

Kilroy remembered the time, the previous winter, when his pod had witnessed a fight between two bull sperm whales for leadership. The combatants had rushed at each other, crashing head-on in collisions that filled the air with spray and made the water tremble, and had finally locked their jaws together and thrashed about until one of them, torn and bleeding, gave up and broke off contact. The winner had rejoined the others, and the loser, wounded and weakened by the struggle, had become an instant victim of the orcas. They rushed in and dispatched him in short order, and the whale, realizing his own helplessness, had offered no resistance. He'd seemed almost glad to get the whole thing over with.

"Are there any fights, or any stragglers?" Kilroy asked.

"No," Morris replied. "They're all just cruising along."

"How big are the young ones?"

"Small, but they're staying pretty close to their mothers."

"Well, let's go have a look. You never can tell."

With Morris leading the way Kilroy increased his speed, and soon he was able to hear the noises of the whales. They were near the surface, swimming slowly and blowing regularly, and there was desultory chatter until they sensed Kilroy's approach. Then one of them sounded the alarm, and he could hear the mothers giving crisp instructions to their young. By the time he had them in sight they were bunched together, and the old bull had positioned himself between Kilroy and the pod. Kilroy circled about, in the faint hope that a young one might dart away from its mother, but the pod kept formation and the bull started toward him, and Kilroy knew his position was hopeless. If he'd had other orcas with him, they could have staged a diversionary attack and possibly separated one of the whales from the pod, but working alone he could accomplish nothing except to put himself in danger of a crushing blow from the bull's flukes. He sounded, leaving Morris circling noisily above, and headed off in search of other food. Morris saw him go and followed along, scanning the horizon for signs of more promising action.

By nightfall, Kilroy was giving serious thought to returning to the aquarium. Life there might be dull, but at least he was fed, and he knew he couldn't last much longer in the ocean without food. Of course his luck might change, and he might fare as well as he did the first day, but if that didn't happen he'd get progressively weaker, until he wouldn't be able to catch anything even if he bumped into it. It was a terrible thought, being unable to feed himself in all those thousands of miles of ocean, but his instinct and training were all based on group feeding, and hunting alone was strictly a hit-or-miss proposition.

"You're out of your mind," Morris said, when Kilroy mentioned the idea of going back. "Just because you're hungry at the end of a day doesn't mean there's no more food in the ocean. Good grief, I'm hungry practically every night."

"You don't have to eat all I do," Kilroy replied. "You can live on scraps."

"They may be scraps to you, but they're like a five-course dinner to me," Morris told him. "I don't eat all that junk because I like it; I eat it because I'm hungry."

But Kilroy was feeling sorry for himself, and wouldn't listen. "Do you know what it takes to keep me alive?" he said. "Just for one day? It takes—"

"I don't give a hoot in a hailstorm what it takes!" Morris cut in. "You're not going to get my sympathy by sitting there and telling me your ideal meal; you're going to get off your fat flukes and hunt for it. I tell you what—if it'll make you feel any better I won't take any more scraps from you, or clean your teeth; I'll let you have every single bite you can catch, if only you'll stop this whining. How does that sound?"

Kilroy was quiet for a moment. "I'm sorry," he said, at last. "I ought to be ashamed of myself."

"That's right," said Morris, rubbing it in. "You ought. You sound more like a spoiled child than like the wolf of the sea. Isn't that what the man called you? Or was it the werewolf?"

"O.K., O.K.," said Kilroy. "I said I'm sorry. I guess I sort of panicked. I won't do it again."

"Good," said Morris. "What's for supper?"

"I'll go look."

"That's more like it," Morris replied, as Kilroy flipped his flukes in the air and headed down.

His sonar told him he was approaching a large mass of something, and in a short while he found himself in the midst of a migrating school of salmon. These fish are hatched in the continental rivers, then move out to sea, and finally return to the rivers of their birth to spawn and die. Their movement is governed by a pattern millions of years old, and they can no more change the pattern than they could grow wings and fly. There were so many of them that Kilroy caught one every time he snapped, and although they scattered and tried to escape there was no way that all of them could avoid him. He ate all he could find, then grabbed one final fish and took it to the surface to Morris.

"Here," he said. "A reward for your patience."

"How did you know?" Morris replied. "It's just what I wanted."

But no matter how hard Kilroy tried, the hunting remained spotty, and there were days when he ate little or nothing. He knew he couldn't keep it up forever but he was not going to admit it to Morris, and his only hope was that, sooner or later, they would run across his old pod. The pod tended to be in the same place at the same time each year, but Kilroy was so young when he was captured that he wasn't fully aware of where he was.

"Where are they most likely to be this time of year?" Morris asked him one evening, at the end of a long day of fruitless searching.

"That's the trouble," Kilroy replied. "I can't be sure. We used to go pretty far north in the summers, then head south before the ice began to close in, and by winter time we'd be well to the south. A good deal of the time, we'd follow the whales."

Morris looked at the sky, and the height of the sun. "Well, we're getting near the end of summer now," he said. "And we've also been heading northwest most of the time, so pretty soon we should meet them on their way south. We don't want to turn around too soon or we'll be ahead of them, so I'd say the best bet is to keep going the way we are, and hope."

"I can't think of anything else," Kilroy replied. "One of these days, they've got to come south."

Just how far north they were became obvious the next day, when Kilroy ran into a pod of beluga, a small white whale that lives mostly in Arctic waters. The beluga were so intent on chasing a school of salmon that they didn't see him, and he was on them in a flash, grabbing one beluga just as it had grabbed a large salmon. For an instant the three animals were joined together like links in a chain, and then gradually Kilroy ate the other two, and went to the surface to take the leftovers to Morris. Morris was so excited he barely noticed the scraps.

"Orca!" he squawked. "There's a pod coming this way!"

Kilroy leaped high out of the water, and in the distance could see the puffs of vapor and the thin, spike-like dorsal fins, and then he could hear the sounds of the approaching orcas. He set off toward them at top speed, and as he got close the lead bull, a thirty-foot-long monster with a towering dorsal fin, came out to meet him.

"What can I do for you?" the bull asked.

"I want to join you!" Kilroy replied. "I've been hunting alone, and I'm almost starved!"

"Where's your pod?" asked the bull.

"I don't know. I was captured last spring, and I haven't seen them since."

"Who captured you?"

"Some men. They put me in an aquarium, and I only just now escaped."

The bull considered this. "That's an unlikely story, if you ask me. How'd you escape?"

"It's too involved to go into now," Kilroy told him. "My friend Morris, the seagull, helped me."

"Come off it," said the bull. "You must think I'll believe anything."

"It's true! Morris will tell you!"

The bull was joined by another male, not quite as big as he, who was probably his son. Kilroy noticed that the rest of the pod consisted of females and their young.

"What's he want?" the younger male asked the bull.

"He wants to join us," the bull replied. "He wants me to believe a seagull helped him escape from an aquarium."

The male looked at Kilroy. "What happened?" he asked. "Were you thrown out of your own pod?"

"No!" Kilroy protested. "I was captured! I'm telling the truth!"

"Look, sonny," the bull said. "We've got enough males here as it is. We don't need any more."

"I won't make any trouble, I promise! I just want to hunt with you!"

"You may not make trouble now, but you will when you're older," the bull told him. "We don't need you, and we don't want you. Now, buzz off."

"But I'll starve!" Kilroy said. "I can't hunt on my own!"

"You heard him," the other male said, crowding close to Kilroy. "Buzz off."

Kilroy looked at the two orcas. For a brief moment he had the idea of challenging them, but either one of them was more than a match for him, and together they could kill him in an instant. He backed away.

"You don't have to shout," he said. "I'm not deaf."

"Then get going," said the younger of the two.

"Look," said Kilroy, with what remained of his pride. "It's a free ocean. I'm not getting in your way, so don't give me any trouble. You were headed south; I'm going north—let's just leave it that way, and save the tough talk for when it's needed. O.K.?"

The others regarded him in silence and he turned and swam off. Morris, who'd been circling overhead, joined him.

"A sweet pair, that," Morris observed. "It would have been a lot of laughs hunting with them."

"I know what I should have told them," Kilroy said. "I should have said they must be pretty unsure of themselves, to think I could cause them any trouble. I should have said—"

"You did just right," Morris cut in. "Don't worry about what you might have said. You let them know they weren't impressing you, and at the same time you gave them no cause to start a fight."

"I was too anxious," Kilroy went on. "I was practically begging them, and that was wrong. I should have offered to help them, instead of asking them to take me in. I should have—"

"Will you listen to me for a minute?" said Morris. "Unless you want to go back and open the whole thing up again, I suggest you forget about it. You came out of it with a whole skin, which is more than I thought you might. I think you can count yourself lucky."

"I just hate to beg," Kilroy said, and lapsed into silence.

They continued northward until, far on the horizon, they saw the sparkling white of the ice, and they knew that Kilroy's pod must be somewhere to the south. They'd been travelling along the migration route of the salmon and as a result had not starved, but this couldn't last forever, and they were aware that unless they found the pod fairly soon they were in trouble. So they headed back to the south, this time closer to shore, on the theory that the pod might be hunting the seals and sea lions and walruses that live along the coastline. But still they saw no other orcas, and Kilroy began to feel the pangs of real hunger.

Then one day he found a piece of a giant squid, most likely torn loose in a fight with a sperm whale, and he was searching around for more scraps when he heard, dimly in the distance, the sounds of orcas. With mounting excitement he headed toward them, and by the time he reached the surface he could see their dorsal fins, perhaps twenty of them, rhythmically appearing and disappearing in groups of four or five at a time. The tall fin of the senior bull veered in his direction, and Kilroy tried to compose himself to make a better showing than he had the last time.

"Looking for something?" the bull asked, and the moment he spoke Kilroy recognized him.

"I'm back!" Kilroy shouted, leaping in the air, and he saw his mother detach herself from the others and come to greet him. He explained what had happened, and how he'd escaped, and he introduced Morris as

80

the one responsible for his freedom. He announced that Morris was to be treated as an honored guest, and two of the younger male orcas, who'd been looking at Morris as a possible between-meals snack, turned away in thinly veiled disgust.

Kilroy had grown enough since his capture so that he no longer needed to stay by his mother; what he needed was to learn how to hunt with the other males, and to this end he was put in a breathing group with one of the younger bulls. He'd forgotten all about the breathing groups, which form an important part of pod life; since orcas have to remember when to breathe (or else fill their lungs with water), they divide into small groups that breathe simultaneously, and this way each group is responsible for its members. This is especially important for the newly born, who have to be taught the basics right away, and it becomes standard pod routine to see that no one orca is breathing by himself. Kilroy took his place and the pod started off, cruising slowly, while Morris flew ahead as advance scout. For the first time in a long while, Kilroy felt that everything was going to be all right.

The difference between hunting alone and hunting with the pod was sharply illustrated next day, when they came across a large school of salmon. The pod immediately divided into two lines, which encircled the school and then, racing around at top speed, compressed the salmon into one mass of confused, frightened fish. Then, one at a time, the orcas darted from the circle into the center, seized what salmon they could, and returned to the rim of the circle, allowing the next orca to lunge in and feed. This continued, with the circle slowly contracting, until every orca had eaten his fill and only a few scattered salmon were left. Then the circle broke, the pod re-formed into its separate breathing groups, and they moved on. It had all been accomplished with the efficiency of a military operation.

The following day Morris returned from scouting far out ahead, and reported a pod of eight blue whales moving slowly southward. The senior bull thought about this, then said, "Any young?"

"No," Morris replied. "They're all big, and bunched pretty well together."

"Well, we'll see what we can do. There's more than one way of going about these things."

The pod increased speed; pretty soon they could hear the whales, and some time later they saw them. The whales were aware of the orcas, and they moved even closer together for mutual protection. At a signal from the bull orca the pod spread out in a line abreast, and followed the whales at a distance. One or two of the younger bulls wanted to attack, but the senior made them stay in formation. The blue whale is the largest animal in the world, and nothing to be attacked lightly. More than three times the size of the largest

orca, it could smash a predator with one blow of its flukes.

For more than an hour the pursuit continued, with the orcas patiently trailing the whales, and then there came the sounds of the whales conferring among themselves. Their conversation didn't last long, and when it was over one of the larger whales, an old bull covered with scars and barnacles, left the pod and dropped back, rolling over and exposing his underside as the orcas caught up with him. It was finished in fairly short order; the other whales swam off, and the male orcas, after first seeing to it that the females and the young were fed, gorged themselves until they could eat no more. Morris was so full he had to ride on Kilroy's head until he'd digested enough to be able once again to fly.

"And to think," he said, as they cruised away from the feeding scene, "you were the one who thought there was no more food in the sea."

"I knew it was there," Kilroy replied. "I just didn't know how to go about getting it."

"I must say, the shore was never like this," said Morris. "I smile when I think of that what's-his-name."

"Who's that?" asked Kilroy.

"You know—the mystic. The gull with the message. I never can remember his name. If he knew there was eating like this, he'd never hack around the seashore again."

Kilroy was quiet for a moment, then said, "I wish people knew about this. I wish there were some way I could tell them."

"There you go, trying to talk to people again," Morris replied. "They're happy the way they are—why not leave them that way?"

"I don't know. I just can't seem to get rid of the idea."

"Well, you think about it all you want. I'm going to think about food."

"So soon? You mean you could eat again?"

Morris spread his wings. "You never can tell," he said. "I'd hate to think that by sitting here I'd missed a chance at a meal." With that he ran along Kilroy's head and took off, and before long was just a dwindling speck against the clouds.

VI

Following the shoreline the pod moved south, until they were well away from the ice. They hunted along the beaches and in bays and estuaries, sometimes lying in wait and ambushing their prey as it emerged into the sea. If they found a place where food was abundant they stayed around, but for the most part they had to keep moving, because the word of their coming spread quickly, and every fish and animal did its best to stay out of their way. The terror inspired by a pod of orcas reduced some animals to helplessness; in others it brought on a desire to flee that deprived the victim of all reason, and in many cases resulted in its almost immediate capture. The older bulls did most of the hunting; they would make the actual attack, then toss the food back to the females and the young, while the junior bulls learned the tactics of the hunt and made occasional kills on their own.

Kilroy found that it was one thing to attack a school of fish in the water; it was quite another thing to charge up to the shore and pick off a seal or sea lion that was trying to scramble to safety, and it was a while before he was able to master the trick. Once, in his rush to the beach, he overdid it and almost became stranded, putting himself at the mercy of a large and belligerent sea lion bull. But he managed to thrash his way back into deep water with only a few cuts and scrapes to show for it, while Morris shrieked himself hoarse overhead. The senior orca looked at him coldly.

"What are you trying to do?" he asked. "Learn to walk?"

"I didn't realize it was so shallow," Kilroy replied. "I was aground before I knew it."

"That's what you have sonar for," the bull told him. "You'll never survive if you don't use all your senses."

"Yes, sir," said Kilroy.

"See that you remember it."

"Yes, sir."

"Whales to seaward!" Morris sang out suddenly. "Bearing due west, distance six miles, headed south!"

The senior bull turned from Kilroy, called the pod away from the beach, and started off to the west. Morris spiralled upward and called down his reports as the whales, sensing the approach of the orcas, changed course. This time, the chase was fruitless. There were no young that could be separated from the pod, and no old ones that would sacrifice themselves, and they maintained too tight a formation to be worth attacking. The orcas tailed along for an hour or so, then spotted a school of mixed tuna and dolphins; they went into their circular attack, and cut the school to pieces. Kilroy thought of how he'd lived before finding the pod, and realized he'd been lucky to survive as long as he had.

One evening, when the shadows were darkening and the light had a tinge of red, they came to the mouth of a bay, and paused. It was a large bay, and possibly a worthwhile hunting ground, but the senior bull didn't want to commit the whole pod when there might be better hunting to seaward. So he sent Kilroy and his breathing group into the bay, with instructions to find out if it looked promising and to report back as soon as possible. The four of them set off, with Morris flying scout, and in short order Morris returned.

"There are men up there," he announced.

"What are they doing?" Kilroy asked. He was suddenly reminded of the place where he'd been captured, and he didn't want to run afoul of any more men and their nets.

"They don't seem to be doing much of anything," Morris replied. "They've got some buildings on the shore, and there are two men sitting out on a pier."

"Any boats?" Kilroy asked.

"A couple at anchor, but nobody's doing anything with them. There's some cooking going on ashore, which probably means they're through for the day." As an afterthought, he added, "They haven't left out any garbage."

Kilroy was considering this when suddenly, in the distance, he heard music. This was not canned music, like that at the aquarium; it was made by a stringed instrument, and in a moment it was joined by another instrument, which made a thin, whistling sound that Kilroy found enchanting. It wasn't orca language, but the whistles were reminiscent of some orcoid phrases, and the combination of the twanging strings and the hollow whistles produced an effect on Kilroy and the others that they'd never felt before. They were drawn toward the sound as though pulled by invisible lines, and their senses were tingling with anticipation. As they neared the source of the music they did what is known as "spying"; they simultaneously put their heads straight up in the air, looked around for four or five seconds, then sank back beneath the surface. What they'd seen was two men on the dock, one of them plucking at an instrument cradled in his arms, and the other blowing into a long tube, which stuck out sideways from his mouth and which he manipulated with the fingers of both hands. Slowly, Kilroy and his group approached the dock, and as they did the men seemed to play with more intensity, an almost frantic note creeping into their music. The four orcas, bewitched by the sounds, slid to the edge of the dock, put their noses out of water, and listened, and they could see beads of moisture forming on the men's foreheads. Finally the men stopped playing; there was total silence for a few seconds, and then the man with the long tube reached down with one hand and touched the top of Kilroy's head. Kilroy didn't move, but the other three slipped beneath the surface and backed away. Kilroy made a few squeaky noises, and the man laughed.

"Trying to sound like a flute?" he said. "All right, see if you can do this." He put the instrument to his mouth and fluttered his fingers as he blew, and a wild series of notes danced in the air and skittered across the water. Kilroy tried to make the same sounds but they didn't come out right, and the man laughed again. "Not bad," he said. "You need a little practice, but so does everybody."

He began to play again, and the man with the stringed instrument joined in, and slowly the other three orcas came back to the dock. They were lying there motionless, listening to the music, when they were interrupted by a raucous cry from above.

"Break it up!" Morris screeched. "Here he comes! Try to look busy!"

Kilroy saw the towering fin of the bull orca coming toward them, and realized they had completely forgotten what they'd come for. They shot away from the dock and went to the bottom, then headed up the bay as fast as they could. When, finally, they came to the surface, the bull was right behind them.

"Where have you been?" he asked.

"Looking around," Kilroy replied.

"Find anything?" The bull stared at him without expression.

"Yes and no," said Kilroy. "We haven't had a chance to cover the whole bay yet."

"What were you doing with those men?"

"You probably won't believe this," Kilroy said, "but they were making sounds like orcas. Or something like."

"What were they saying?"

"That's what we were trying to figure out. It was close, but nothing we could actually understand."

"That's right," said another of the group. "I've never heard anything like it. One man even touched Kilroy on the head."

90

The bull regarded them in silence for a moment, then said, "Now should we start looking for food?"

"Yes, *sir*," they replied in one voice, and off they all went.

When the orcas had disappeared, the two men walked from the dock back to the main cabin. It was almost dark, and everything had been secured for the night.

"That's the closest I've ever seen them come," said the man with the guitar. "It was almost as though they'd been trained."

"I think the one I touched *had* been trained," the flute man replied. "It spooked the others, but he seemed to like it."

"Well, if he hadn't liked it you can be sure he wouldn't have let you do it," said the first. "Either that, or we'd now be calling you Lefty."

"That's not what I meant. I meant he liked it so much I got the feeling he was asking me to do it. Or maybe I'm reading too much into it."

"Wouldn't you know they'd come at a time when we didn't have the gear set up. If we could've picked them up on the hydrophones, we might have got something really good."

"I don't know. The mechanical business is good as far as it goes, but it's not the answer."

"Do you know a better one?"

The flute man thought for a while, then said, "The best way is to do it in person. They prefer live music to the canned stuff, so personal contact should be better than fooling around with recordings."

"So you're going to turn into an orca?"

"That would be the ideal way."

"Well, good luck. I can't wait to see your new teeth."

"If I can't actually turn into an orca, at least I can work at their level."

"You mean swimming?"

"No, I mean in the kayak. Go out in the kayak and mix with them, and see what happens. Try to make some sort of contact."

They had reached the hut, and as they opened the door they were greeted by the smells of a wood fire, hot coffee, and roasting meat. Three other men were in the room, one tending the fire and the other two puttering with elaborate mechanical devices.

"Guess what!" the guitar man announced, in a loud voice. "Charlie's engaged!" The others looked up in surprise, and he went on, "The most beautiful orca in the world just snuggled up to him, and he's eloping with the pod. We'll have to give him a going-away shower."

"Very funny," Charlie said, putting his flute on his bunk.

"Harry, you've been away from civilization too long," the cook said. "You ought to go back to the university."

"Not until after Charlie's wedding," Harry replied. "I'm ring bearer."

"Is it all right to ask what this is all about?" one of the other men said. He was older than the rest, and his beard was speckled with white.

"You tell them, Charlie," said Harry. "It's your idea."

Charlie took a deep breath. "We were playing music out on the dock," he said. "These four orcas came up, apparently attracted by the sound, and one of them let me touch his head. He had no fear at all, but the others were a little spooky. It occurred to me if I got in the kayak and went out and joined them, I might get close enough to make some sort of contact. I don't know— I just got the feeling this one guy wanted something more. He tried to imitate my flute."

"They can be trained to do anything," the older man said. "You know that as well as I do."

"I know, but he did this on his own. I didn't train him to do a thing."

"Once you make contact, then what?"

"Who knows? But I can't lose anything by trying."

"Only your life," another man said. "I wouldn't go among those things in a kayak for anything in the world."

"You're an engineer, not a biologist," Charlie told him. "You don't know about animals."

"And I intend to keep it that way. Animals are interested only in food, and you're not going to catch me being hors d'oeuvre for a pod of orcas."

"You needn't worry—engineers make notoriously bad eating. They're all full of nuts and bolts and wheels."

"That's nothing to what you're full of."

"All right, all right," the older man broke in. "Let's keep it scientific, should we? We've only got two more weeks, and then we can pack it up for the winter."

"And not a moment too soon," said the engineer. "It's going to take me all winter to sort out my tapes."

Next morning Charlie went up a hill behind the camp, where he could look in all directions for any signs of the orcas. The surface of the bay was calm and unruffled, and off to seaward the ocean lay like a giant slab of slate. The air was cold, and some of the trees had turned yellow and orange, and he knew that winter wasn't far away. Perhaps the pod had already moved on, but the idea of being among them appealed to him so strongly that he took his flute, put the kayak in the water, and got in. The kayak was a one-man canoe, decked over to make it waterproof, with an apron around the cockpit and drawstrings to secure it to the paddler. A man who was tightly laced into his kayak could roll it completely over and come up without having taken on a drop of water. Charlie put his flute down the front of his shirt, took the two-bladed paddle, and moved quietly out into the bay.

He headed toward the ocean, on the theory that the orcas would not have stayed long in the bay, and after about a half hour he laid the paddle across the deck in front of him, took out his flute, and began to play. Nothing happened for several minutes, and then four orcas came to the surface directly ahead of him, and began to move closer. From the markings and the shape of the dorsal fin he recognized Kilroy as one, and he played directly to Kilroy as the orcas circled the kayak. Then as though leading the way, they started off, slowly enough so he could follow them, and Charlie took his paddle and moved with them, taking

no notice of the fact that a seagull was hovering over-head wherever he went. After a while the orcas stopped, and waited, and once more Charlie took his flute and played for them. This brought three more to the surface, and they joined the others in escorting Charlie out to sea. He was so intent on the orcas that he failed to realize how far he'd come; all he knew was that they were trying to lead him into their pod, and he would gladly have followed them across the ocean if necessary. Each time he stopped to play his flute more orcas appeared, until he felt he must be paddling in a sea full of them, but only Kilroy came really close to the kayak. The others formed a line ahead of it, dropping back only when Charlie stopped to play, whereas Kilroy stayed always within arm's reach, squeaking and clicking and trying to imitate the flute.

Then, suddenly, the orcas were gone. One moment they were all around, and the next moment there was nothing but ripples to show where they'd been. Faintly, in the distance, Charlie heard the puttering of a motorboat, and as it got louder he could see Harry at the controls, leaning forward as though to give the boat more speed. A wild anger came over him, as though he'd been awakened from a particularly beau-tiful dream, and when the boat came alongside he shook his flute at Harry.

"Nice going!" he shouted. "If you really wanted to drive them away, why didn't you shoot at them with a cannon?"

"Do you know how far out you are?" Harry replied. "Have you taken a look at the shoreline recently?"

"I don't know, and I don't care! All I know is you've

scattered them all over the ocean!"

"Well, in another hour *you*'d have been scattered all over the ocean. Take a look at those storm clouds."

Charlie looked where Harry indicated, and saw heavy clouds piling up along the horizon. He said nothing as he handed his flute and paddle to Harry, then loosened his drawstrings and climbed from the kayak into the motorboat. Between them they brought the kayak aboard, then Harry headed back toward shore. They reached the pier just as the wind-driven rain began to slash across the surface of the water.

By nighttime the storm had passed. Black, shredded bits of cloud flew past the treetops like hurrying witches, and through the thicker clouds above there came an occasional glow from the moon. Charlie went outside to smell the clean, rain-washed air, and above the sighing of the wind in the pines he could hear the distant rumble of surf. The bay was as black as the ocean depths, and without the moon it was impossible to see the pier and the nearby boats. All at once, above the noise of the trees, Charlie heard the explosive puff of orcas coming up to breathe, and he frantically scanned the surface of the bay without seeing anything. Then came the puff again, and once more, and in the quiet that followed he saw a phosphorescent ring begin to form in the water beyond the pier. It grew brighter and brighter, until he could see it was the wake of four orcas, following one another in a whirling circle, and then they broke off and swam quietly away, leaving behind them a luminous O that grew gradually dimmer and faded from sight. Charlie waited for them to reappear but they didn't; they didn't even come up to breathe until they were out of his hearing. He strained his eyes to see if anything remained of the O, but it had vanished as completely as the orcas, and he began to wonder if he'd seen it at all. But there had been no mistaking it, or what had caused it, and as he went back to the hut he tried to reason out what had been in the orcas' minds. The fact that they'd left so quietly, making no visible wake other than the O, showed they knew what they were doing; they were leaving a message, or a symbol, for him to see, and it was up to him to interpret what it meant. He tried to fit the O into an English word but realized this was insane: the orcas knew neither English nor how to spell, so the letter had to mean something to them alone. But what? Would it signify the circle they swam in while rounding up fish? Unlikely. The symbol of perfection? The earth? The sun? The universe? Cut it out, he told himself; you'll drive yourself crazy. There's got to be a simpler explanation. Put yourself in an orca's place—what would a circle mean to you? An eye? An egg? No—an egg isn't round. A—a blowfish? Don't be stupid. Hey, a fish egg *is* round. But an orca isn't a fish. CUT IT OUT! KEEP IT SIMPLE!

It was in this mood of confused frustration that he opened the door to the hut and went inside. Harry looked up at him.

"What's the weather doing?" Harry asked.

"O," said Charlie. "What does O mean to you?"

Harry looked at him queerly. "O what?" he said. "O say can you see?"

"Just O. The orcas gave me an O."

"Sit down, Charlie," said the man with the white-speckled beard. "How do you feel?"

"I feel fine. It's the orcas I'm thinking about."

"Headaches? Dizzy spells? Spots before the eyes? Shortness of breath?"

"I said I'm fine!"

"Sure you are, Charlie. Tell us about the orcas."

"I was up on the hill, and four of them came into the bay and swam in a circle in front of the dock, making a big phosphorescent O. Then they went away very quietly, so as not to disturb the circle. It lasted for almost a minute—well, half a minute. Fifteen seconds."

"Then what did they do?"

"That's all! I just want to know what they meant!"

"If they'd done two more circles," Harry observed, "it would have meant no hits, no runs, no errors."

"Maybe they were trying to draw a wheel," the engineer put in. "Did they make a hub in the middle of it?"

"No!" Charlie replied, almost shouting. "They just made an O, and then left!"

The engineer shrugged. "Illiterate, probably," he said. "I'll bet they don't know any other letters. If they'd started with an M, and gone on to spell 'mother,' then you'd have something to work on. But an O—" he shrugged again— "they probably did it by mistake."

"It was no mistake!" said Charlie, by this time red-faced with rage. "They were trying to tell me something!"

"I once saw a turtle spell out the Gettysburg address," the fourth man said. "He did it by dragging his tail through the sand. Had pretty neat writing, too. Old-fashioned script, with all the curlycues."

Charlie reached for something to throw, but the older man restrained him. "Take it easy," he said. "You've been working too hard. Just relax, and think about something else. Things will look different tomorrow."

"I hope he got the signal," Kilroy said, as he and the other orcas swam off to rejoin the pod.

"Are you sure he was there?" asked the one nearest him.

"Yes, he was up on the hill," Kilroy replied. "It couldn't have been anyone else."

"But will he understand it?"

"I don't know how he could miss. It was a simple greeting, so if he saw it he must have understood it."

VII

The pod continued south, following the migration of larger marine life away from the Arctic areas. Air-breathing animals, such as orcas and whales and porpoises, must stay well away from the ice floes, because a sudden heavy freeze can trap them beneath the surface and prevent their breathing. They can keep air holes open for just so long, and then they drown.

Also, the warmer waters are better for the birth of the young, who can be more easily cared for during the crucial first days of their lives. Kilroy witnessed the birth of a baby orca, and watched with fascination as it slowly emerged, tail first, from the birth canal, while other females hovered protectively nearby. The moment it was free they nudged it to the surface, where it could take its first breath, and from then on its mother supervised its breathing and feeding. Its first attempt to find her nipples was a trial-and-error affair that took some little time, but once having found them, it was never in doubt again. It stayed close at her side, touching her for the sense of protection it gave, and feeding whenever the mood was upon it. All orcas tend to swim close together, often touching one another, but this calf stayed so close to its mother it might have been part of her skin. As it grew it began to leave her side for a quick frolic or two, jumping in the air for the sheer fun of it, but it never went very far and it always came back to her side. Kilroy, who felt a certain proprietary interest because of having witnessed the birth, tried once or twice to get close enough to teach it a few tricks, but the mother made it quite clear he wasn't welcome, and after a while he gave up. Morris was interested in the whole procedure, although he made it clear he thought the egg method far superior.

"I mean, you break the shell and that's that," he said, to Kilroy. "What could be simpler?"

"You still have to learn to fly," Kilroy replied. "We learn to breathe, you learn to fly."

"I never thought of it that way," said Morris. "As far as I can remember, I've always known how."

"And your mother had to feed you," Kilroy went on. "She brought you food she'd found, and you picked it out of her craw."

Morris was quiet for a moment. "I still think the egg system is better," he said. "It's neater, somehow."

"Well, don't look at me," said Kilroy. "There's nothing *I* can do about it."

"I'm not being personal," Morris replied, quickly. "In fact I think it's interesting, to see how others live. I'd never have known about this, if I'd stayed with those gulls."

"Well, I wouldn't be here now," said Kilroy. "So we each have gained something."

"It makes you think, doesn't it?" Morris said.

102

"Not much," replied Kilroy. "I have other things on my mind." And with that he and his group sounded, to check out a sonar contact.

The mating season of the sperm whales reached its peak in early spring, and twice Kilroy and his pod saw the battle between the bulls for leadership. The sperm whale pod was, in a sense, like a harem, and the leader had as many wives as he wanted. This was also true with orcas—although the orca family ties were stronger than those of the whales—and the senior bull orca had the final say as to who his wives were. This, Kilroy realized, was why he'd been kept out of the pod he'd tried to join; the two bulls would eventually have to fight for supremacy, and they didn't want a third party around to complicate matters.

The first sperm whale fight was a thundering affair that went on for almost an hour, and while the older whale was clearly the winner he didn't damage the challenger enough for the orcas to finish him off. The minute they closed in, the whales clustered together in a defensive group, and both the senior bull and his defeated rival were still in an ugly enough humor to be dangerous. Two or three of the orcas darted in and tried to bite the whales in a vulnerable spot, but their attacks were unsuccessful and after a while they gave up.

The second fight was just the opposite. The combatants charged each other repeatedly, using their heads as monstrous battering rams, then locked their jaws together and settled down to a test of strength. They were so preoccupied that they didn't notice the orcas, who divided into two groups, one for each whale, and came charging in and attacked them simultaneously.

103

The orcas hit the undersides first, opening up great wounds that drained the strength of the already depleted whales, and then they swarmed all over their victims and started their feast. Morris, from his position high in the air, saw the rest of the whale pod move hurriedly away as soon as it became clear that neither bull had survived.

Finally, as winter drew to a close and the days became longer, they started to move north. Kilroy wondered, every now and then, if the same men would be in the bay as before, and he determined that, if they were, he'd make one more try at getting through to them. He'd seemed so close with the man in the kayak that he couldn't believe there wasn't some way to do it, but without intelligent cooperation from the men it would be much harder. In his experience most men had ideas of their own, and were unwilling to relax long enough to consider new ones. They seemed to live by rules rather than feeling, and this made communication difficult.

On their way north they had an experience that made a deep impression on the other orcas, and gave Kilroy an added flicker of hope. They were off the coast, close enough to land so they could see the lights of the large cities at night, and in the distance they saw a ship putting out to sea. They usually avoided large ships, which made so much commotion in the water that they frightened everything except dolphins into leaving the area, but there was something different about this ship: in addition to the engine and propeller noises they could hear, faintly but distinctly, the sounds of music. Fascinated, they went closer, and realized that this was live music, made by a number of different instruments all playing together. The combination of sounds into one harmonious whole was something none of them had heard before, and they closed in on the ship quietly, without their usual chatter, in order to inspect the source of the sound. Silently, in single file, they went past, and were able to see that a number of men were gathered on the afterdeck, making music, while other people moved about. At the sight of the orcas many people came to the rail to stare, but the musicians kept playing, and the orcas turned and circled the ship. Then a half dozen of the younger males—Kilroy and his group among them—formed a line abreast and followed the ship on the surface, while the others continued to circle around it, periodically diving and surfacing in a form of unison governed by the music.

Then the senior bull, apparently feeling that such levity was inappropriate, ordered the pod to break off and continue on their way, and they re-formed as they had been before. They went north, and the ship went west, and when darkness fell they could still see its lights on the horizon.

A heavy spring fog had settled along the coast, and the men at the research station moved in a damp, white world of their own. The fog muffled all sound, and only certain, isolated noises could be heard: the creaking cry of a seagull, the faint splash of a fish jumping in the bay, and the far-off moan of a coastal foghorn. Over the winter, the engineer had spliced together the best tapes they'd made of orca conversation, and although machines had analyzed the sounds, and made graphs of their frequencies, modulations, and tonal characteristics, nobody knew what they meant, beyond a rather vague guess at the conditions under which they were uttered. As an experiment the engineer had tried to reproduce an orca sound mechanically, and while he was aware it wasn't perfect he was interested in seeing if he could get an orca to reply to it. If he could do that, he felt, he had the first step toward rational communication. This was the project for which the university had given them a grant, and so far their results had been discouraging.

One morning, after breakfast, Charlie took his flute up on the hill and began to play. It was the fifth straight day of fog, and with the station's activities curtailed Charlie felt the beginnings of cabin fever creeping over him. He sat, cross-legged like an Indian, on the damp ground and let his frustration pour out through his flute, feeling better with every note he uttered. He played "Tales From the Vienna Woods," and "The Stars and Stripes Forever," and Brahms' "Lullaby," and Beethoven's "Moonlight Sonata," and "The Washington Post March," and ended up with "Our Director," "She'll Be Comin' 'Round the Mountain," and "Mrs. Robinson." When, finally, he stopped for breath, he felt relaxed and vaguely pleased with himself, and he was trying to think of something else to play when out of the fog came the unmistakable sound of orcas blowing. Charlie stood up, listening, and when they blew again he ran down the hill, dragged the kayak out of the boat shed, and got in and paddled off, without telling anyone he was going. He realized, as the fog enveloped him, that this was a stupid thing to do, because he'd brought neither compass, chart, nor food, but he was so intent on meeting the orcas that everything else seemed unimportant. All he could see was the water immediately surrounding him; the rest of the world was a white nothing.

He stopped, every now and then, to play a few notes on his flute, and then suddenly he heard a blast of air nearby, and four orcas were looking at him. They repeated the routine of the previous fall; they swam off slowly enough for him to follow, and gradually they led him out to the pod. Orcas were blowing on all sides, some stopping to listen to the music and some going under again on business of their own. It was frustrating for Charlie to be able to see them only on the surface; he felt he should get in the water and swim around with them, but lacking any diving gear he knew this was impossible. So he had to settle for what was figuratively a seat in the bleachers, and observe them only as they decided to come to him. He recognized Kilroy, who had grown since their last meeting but was easy to tell by his markings (the white spot on his back, behind his dorsal fin, looked like a map of Africa, and there was a slight hook at the tip of his fin), and Kilroy came so close to the kayak that Charlie was able to reach out and touch him. Charlie remembered hearing that among the northern Indians one test of bravery was to find an orca sleeping on the surface, approach him quietly in a canoe, then have one man leap from the canoe, run along the orca's back to his head, and jump back into the canoe. The man who could do that was much admired by his people, and for a moment Charlie was tempted to try the same trick. But then he remembered he was alone; even if Kilroy let him run along his back he'd never be able to return to the kayak, and he was too far out to risk having to swim. So instead he simply talked to Kilroy, making noises that he hoped sounded something like orca language, and Kilroy swam placidly by his side, not reacting to the noises but seemingly content with Charlie's company.

Then, spurred by some signal or noise unknown to Charlie, the orcas vanished, and he was left alone in his pocket of fog. He waited for them to return but they didn't, and after a few minutes he decided he'd better start heading back toward land. But without a compass he had no idea where the land lay; he was far enough from the bay so he couldn't hear the foghorn, and for an instant panic began to nibble at his nerve ends. His first instinct was to paddle frantically in any direction, but he knew this would only drain his strength and get him nowhere, and his alternative was to wait, looking and listening, and hope the tide would carry him to some spot along the coast. How long this might take was anybody's guess, and without food or water he could be in for an unpleasant time. He vowed never to take the kayak out again without a compass; he'd leave one in it at all times and also leave some emergency rations, but all these resolves did him no good at the moment; he was alone in a fog-bound stretch of ocean, with nothing to do but wait and hope for the fog to burn off.

To pass the time he picked up his flute again, and

played a few pieces he thought appropriate to the occasion. He played "Song of the Volga Boatmen," "Anchors Aweigh," "Barnacle Bill the Sailor," and "On a Slow Boat to China," and he was just starting "My Bonnie Lies Over the Ocean" when Kilroy and his three companions appeared in a line abreast ahead of the kayak, and moved off slowly on the surface. Charlie picked up his paddle and followed them, and they continued on the surface for perhaps a half hour until, very faintly, he could hear the distant groan of the foghorn. He headed toward it and the orcas disappeared, and then, almost as though a curtain had been raised, he found himself in bright sunlight, with the ocean sparkling all around him and a dark line of trees marking the land ahead. Behind him the fog bank towered like a massive iceberg, and he knew if it hadn't been for Kilroy he would still be out there, drifting aimlessly with the tide.

Harry was on the dock when he returned, and before Harry could say anything Charlie shouted, "They're out there! There must be fifty of them!"

"Fifty what?" replied Harry.

"Fifty orcas! A whole big pod!"

"Where'd you find them—Los Angeles?"

"They're right out there! They can't be more than a mile or so away!" Charlie knew it was considerably more than a mile, but he saw no reason to admit how far he'd gone. The fog bank was now about three miles off, so he must have been farther out than he cared to think about. "They're the same ones as last year," he continued, as he brought the kayak alongside the dock. "I recognized that one we played the music for."

"And I suppose he recognized you," Harry said, taking Charlie's flute and paddle from him.

"As a matter of fact, he did," Charlie replied.

They lifted the kayak out of the water in silence, and then Harry said, "The boss would have a word with you."

"About what?" Charlie asked, feeling sure he knew.

"He didn't tell me," replied Harry. "He just said if you ever got back, he'd like to talk to you."

The head scientist was the older man with the white-flecked beard, and when Charlie came into the hut the man took him off to one side. "Look, Charlie," he said, quietly, "I don't like to make any rules around here, but there are a few things I think—"

"I'm sorry," Charlie cut in. "I know just what you mean, and I won't do it again." He had figured, on his way to the hut, that the best defense was to start right off by admitting his error, then take the subject elsewhere. "There was no excuse for it except I got carried away, but I think I may have found something important."

"What's that?" the boss asked, glad not to have to finish his speech.

"There's a whole pod out there—the same ones we saw last year—and they recognized me. I think if we can lure them into the bay we can play back some of the tapes we made of them, and see how they react to their own voices."

The older man thought a moment. "Possibly," he said. "How far out are they?"

"Well—they're moving around," Charlie replied. "It's hard to be sure where they are at any given time.

110

But I've found that music will bring them, and if we combine that with some of the tapes—well—who knows?"

"I guess it's worth trying," the boss said. "I don't see what we can lose."

So they set up the underwater hydrophones and played tapes of musical numbers, alternating with recordings of the orcas' noises, but not even one fin broke the surface of the water. With the listening gear the men could occasionally hear the distant sounds of orcas, but no matter what they did they couldn't attract the animals to their station. Then the engineer had an idea.

"I know this is a long shot," he said, "but let's try that fake orca noise I put together—the mechanical one."

"If real orca noises won't draw them, why should that?" Harry asked. "That sounds about as much like an orca as I do."

"Have you any better ideas?" the engineer replied. "We've tried everything else."

Harry looked at Charlie. "Maybe we should let the Orca Kid, here, swim out and herd them in," he said. "He's the only one they pay attention to."

"Give me some scuba gear, and I'll do it," Charlie replied. "I wished I'd had it with me this morning."

"I think we'd best keep him close to shore," the boss said. "Let's try the mechanical one, and see what happens."

They played the engineer's orca imitation once, and then again, and then a third time, but nothing happened. This was not surprising since nobody had ex-

pected anything—except the engineer, who had se-
cretly hoped for a reaction of some sort—and they
were discussing what to try next when suddenly,
twenty yards offshore, Kilroy's fin broke the surface
and his grinning head appeared, and he made a noise
that was an exact copy of the mechanical one, flaws
and all. Then he sounded, leaving the men staring,
dumbfounded, at the ring of ripples where he'd been.
It was several moments before anyone spoke.

"He did it!" the engineer said, at last. "He answered
me!"

"He didn't answer *you*, dum-dum," Harry replied.
"He was mocking your recording."

"But he answered!" the engineer insisted. "He
knew what he was doing!"

"Of course he knew what he was doing. You'd know
what you were doing if you barked like a dog, but that
wouldn't mean you were talking to a dog."

"Play it again!" said the engineer. "Do it once more,
and see what happens!"

They played it again, and twice more, but nothing
happened, and they finally gave up. The engineer remained firm in his belief that Kilroy had been answer-
ing him, but the others were more impressed by the
fact Kilroy had imitated the obvious flaws in the tape.
This showed that he knew what they were trying to do,
and was . . . Was what? Giving them encouragement?
Mocking them? Making a mindless echo of a meaningless noise? That was the question, but it seemed to
show a critical faculty that nobody had, until now,
associated with orcas. It was as though a new door had

112

been opened a crack, and they were trying to peek through to the other side.

That night, after supper, Charlie went to the hill behind the camp. The moon was full, brightening the landscape like a thin dusting of snow, and the bay sparkled in its reflected light. The fir trees cast shadows on the water as black as forest pools, but everything else gave off a quiet glow. Charlie played a few numbers on his flute, and for a while he forgot about orcas and imagined he was a shepherd back in the hills of ancient Greece. On a night like this, when the moonlight played tricks with the shadows, it would be perfectly possible to see fauns and satyrs and woodland nymphs, and he closed his eyes and pictured the creatures of mythology dancing around him. He felt a curious attraction to the moon, and even through closed eyes he could see its light and feel its gravitational pull. He knew that the full moon makes animals do strange and unusual things, and the longer he played his flute the more he felt his kinship to the animals, as though every living thing were the same in the light of the moon.

Finally, feeling slightly dizzy, he opened his eyes, and when he looked down at the bay he saw, dimly at first, the same luminous O he'd seen before. Slowly it became brighter, outshining even the reflected moonlight, and Charlie raced down the hill to the camp, shouting, "They're here! They're here! They're making the O again!" Then he heard himself adding, "They're making the O for orca!" and immediately felt silly.

113

The others came tumbling out of the hut and followed him up to where they could look down on the bay, but by the time they got there the O was no more than a faint circle that faded quickly and was gone. There was a short silence.

"It was there!" Charlie said. "I saw it—I swear I did!"

Harry drew a deep breath, and let it out slowly. "Look, pal," he said. "Would you ask them to give us some warning next time? If they'll honk twice before they start, then I won't have to run all the way up this hill for nothing."

"It could have been a trick of the moonlight," the engineer put in. "I can see almost anything I want to out there."

"It was no trick of anything!" Charlie replied. "They were making the same circle they made before!"

"Look there," said the older man. "Is that what you mean?"

They all looked as a new circle began to form, to the left of where the first one had been, and as it grew brighter their eyes widened in astonishment.

"That's it!" Charlie shouted. "They're doing it again!"

There was total silence on the hill as the orcas made their second O, and when, finally, they swam away and it faded, the men found they'd been holding their breaths. They waited to see if a third O would appear, but it didn't; instead, they heard the distant sounds of many orcas blowing.

"Turn on the tapes!" the boss said, for the first time

showing excitement. The engineer ran down and turned on the hydrophones, and the sounds of orca chatter could be clearly heard. They were talking with greater intensity than ever before, and the engineer ran back up the hill and joined the others as a whole parade of orcas, blowing and leaping in formation, came up the bay. Spontaneously, the men began to clap and cheer and shout; they jumped in unison with the orcas, and the orcas called and whistled and honked, while Charlie, bounding in the air like a gazelle, tried to make music on his flute. Each group was imitating the noises of the other and both groups were leaping as though directed by a single hand, and for a few minutes there occurred a wild ballet in the light of the moon in which both men and animals were alike. There was a bond between them that transcended language, and a shared enthusiasm for something undefinable that bordered on mass hysteria. The men were the more undisciplined of the two groups; they lost all control and did whatever came into their minds, whereas the orcas, although unrestrained, seemed to have a better knowledge of what they were doing. If anyone was in charge, it was the orcas.

The parade, with one noisy seagull flying overhead, went past the station, then turned back out to sea, leaving a half dozen men sitting, limp and stunned, on the ground. One by one they got up, dusted off their hands, and wandered down toward the station, where the hydrophones were recording the sounds of the departing orcas. Nobody spoke for the rest of the evening, and by the time the orca sounds had faded into silence the men were either asleep, or staring into the darkness above their bunks.

"I wish I'd been born an orca," Morris said, next day, when the pod was cruising slowly off the coast. "Gulls could never get people to do tricks like that."

"I'm not quite sure how we did it," Kilroy replied. "It just seemed to happen."

"Well, whatever it was it could never happen with gulls. Our language is a real mess."

"It isn't the language so much," Kilroy told him. "It's that you have the same feeling. All of a sudden this feeling is there, and that's all there is to it."

"What's the feeling?"

"I don't know. . . . Being free. . . . Sharing the same world. . . . I can't explain it more than that."

Morris shook his head. "I don't see gulls in a situation like that. Gulls'd be fighting about something before the feeling ever got off the ground."

"You never can tell. It does strange things."

"To you, maybe. That's why I wish I'd been born an orca."

Kilroy tried to think of a way to change Morris' mood. "If you were, then you couldn't be hatched out of an egg," he said. "You'd have to be born in water, like the rest of us."

Morris considered this. "If I thought I could do it, I would," he said. "You don't know how lucky you are."

And with that he rose in the air, made a climbing turn, and soon was out of sight.